國家圖書館出版品預行編目(CIP)資料

基礎泰文拼讀:從發音到短句的系統學習 /
時時泰泰語資源中心作. -- 一版. --
新北市:時時泰工作室, 2025.05
面; 17x26 公分
ISBN 978-626-98501-8-1(平裝)
1.CST: 泰語 2.CST: 讀本
803.758 114007113

《基礎泰文拼讀 - 從發音到短句的系統學習》
編　　　輯 時時泰泰語資源中心
插　　　圖 illustrations designed by Canva
錄　　　音 กิพนาถ สุดจิตต์
泰 文 校 對 Isabella Happe / ดีดี้
專 案 經 理 Emily Chen
審　　　訂 กิพนาถ สุดจิตต์
出　　　版 時時泰工作室
　　　　　 234 新北市永和區秀朗路一段 90 巷 8 號
　　　　　 (02) 8921-2198
泰 文 音 檔 請到Podcast/ soundon 搜尋「時時泰工作室」
課 本 網 站 https://www.everthai.tw/
社 群 連 結 https://portaly.cc/everthaistudio
出 版 日 期 2025 年 5 月一版初刷
定　　　價 350 元

I　S　B　N 978-626-98501-8-1
I S B N 978-626-98501-9-8 (EPUB)
總　經　銷 紅螞蟻圖書有限公司
地　　　址 114台北市內湖區舊宗路2段121巷19號
電　　　話 (02) 2795-3656
傳　　　真 (02) 2795-4100

欲利用本書全部或部分內容者,
須徵得作者同意或書面授權。
請洽時時泰工作室:everthailand2019@gmail.com

Thai Phonics Fundamentals: A Systematic Journey from
Pronunciation to Short SentencesPublished by EverThai Studio
Printed in Taiwan
Copyright © EverThai Studio
ALL RIGHTS RESERVED

時時泰工作室| 泰語學習與跨文化交流領導品牌

序
Preface

學習一門新語言，猶如打開一扇通往另一個文化世界的大門。泰語，作為泰國的官方語言，不僅是日常溝通的工具，更是泰國文化、傳統與生活方式的載體。對於初學者來說，泰語的獨特之處在於其聲調系統與拼讀規則，這往往是學習的最大挑戰，但也正是它的魅力所在。正如泰國的一句諺語所說：「ช้า ๆ ได้พร้าเล่มงาม (慢工出細活)」，意思是只要有耐心，循序漸進，就能獲得美好的成果。這句諺語不僅適用於生活，也同樣適用於學習泰語的旅程。

《基礎泰文拼讀 - 從發音到短句的系統學習》旨在為初學者提供一個結構清晰、循序漸進的學習路徑。本書從泰語拼讀的基礎開始，逐步帶領讀者掌握中音子音、高音子音、低音子音與母音的發音規則，並進一步熟悉聲調的應用，最終過渡到短句的拼讀練習。本書的設計理念是「由淺入深，循序漸進」。每章節都包含拼讀練習與選擇題，幫助學習者反覆練習，鞏固發音與詞彙的記憶。無論您是完全的初學者，還是希望複習泰語拼讀基礎的學習者，這本書都能成為您學習路上的好幫手。

學習泰語需要耐心與恆心，但當您能夠流利拼讀單字、朗讀短句，甚至用泰語與人交流時，您會發現所有的努力都是值得的。讓我們一起開始這段泰語學習的旅程吧！正如泰國諺語所說，慢慢來，您一定能打造出屬於自己的「漂亮之刀」——流利的泰語能力！

時時泰工作室
2025年5月

時時泰工作室 | 泰語學習與跨文化交流領導品牌

目錄
Contents

本書規則	1
組成	2
母音	3-4
子音	5-11
尾音	12
拼讀規則一：中音子音＋母音	13-16
拼讀規則一：高音子音＋母音	17-20
拼讀規則三：低音子音＋母音	21-28
拼讀規則四：簡化母音	29
拼讀規則五：聲調符號	30-33
泰語規則六：前引字	34-38
基礎泰文拼讀練習	39
中音子音＋母音 練習一：拼讀練習	40-41
中音子音＋母音 練習二：選擇題	42-43
高音子音＋母音 練習一：拼讀練習	44-45
高音子音＋母音 練習二：選擇題	46-47
低音子音＋母音 練習一：拼讀練習	48-49
低音子音＋母音 練習二：選擇題	50-51
尾音與簡化母音 練習一：拼讀練習	52-53
尾音與簡化母音 練習二：選擇題	54-55
聲調 練習一：拼讀練習	56-58
聲調 練習二：選擇題	59-61
前引字 練習一：拼讀練習	62-64
前引字 練習二：選擇題	65-67
短句拼讀一：拼讀練習	68-76
短句拼讀二：拼讀練習	77-86
練習題答案	87-99

時時泰工作室｜泰語學習與跨文化交流領導品牌

本書規則
Preface

1. 本書在音標上以「:」來標示長母音。
2. 本書在聲調上以數字「12345」來標示泰語聲調。

第一聲	第二聲	第三聲	第四聲	第五聲
First Tone	Second Tone	Third Tone	Fourth Tone	Fifth Tone
กา	ก่า	ก้า	ก๊า	ก๋า
ka : 1	ka : 2	ka : 3	ka : 4	ka : 5

3. 本書 MP3 音檔,請掃 QRcode 到 Podcast 上聆聽。
4. 歡迎一起來追蹤「時時泰工作室」

1. This book uses ":" to indicate long vowels in phonetics.

2. This book uses the numbers "12345" to represent Thai tones.

3. To access the MP3 audio files of this book, please scan the QR code to listen on the Podcast.

4. Feel free to follow "EverThai Studio" for more updates.

| 官方網站 | Line@帳號 | Thread |
| 蝦皮Shopee | Portaly | Podcast |

時時泰工作室 | 泰語學習與跨文化交流領導品牌

組成
Composition of Thai

根據泰國皇家學院規範，中部方言被定為現代標準泰語。目前泰語字母包含44個子音、32個母音、4個聲調符號（共5個聲調）及8組尾音。泰語屬於拼音文字，由母音、子音、尾音和聲調組成，基本拼字規則為母音加子音。泰文字母類似中文的ㄅㄆㄇ或英文的ABC，只要熟記母音和子音，學習拼字會更加輕鬆！泰語的聲調對於語意有重要影響，同一個詞彙因聲調不同可能有完全不同的意思。因此，學習泰語時，掌握聲調是關鍵。此外，泰語的書寫方向為從左到右，單詞之間不加空格，需依語境判斷分詞。熟悉基本拼音規則後，理解泰語文法會更加順暢。

The Royal Institute of Thailand designates the Central Thai dialect as modern Standard Thai, comprising 44 consonants, 32 vowels, 4 tone markers (5 total tones), and 8 final consonant groups. Thai is a phonetic script where tones significantly impact meaning, making tone mastery essential. Similar to English and Chinese phonetics, once vowels and consonants are learned, spelling becomes easier. Thai is written left to right without spaces between words, relying on context for understanding. Familiarity with phonetic rules aids in grasping Thai grammar.

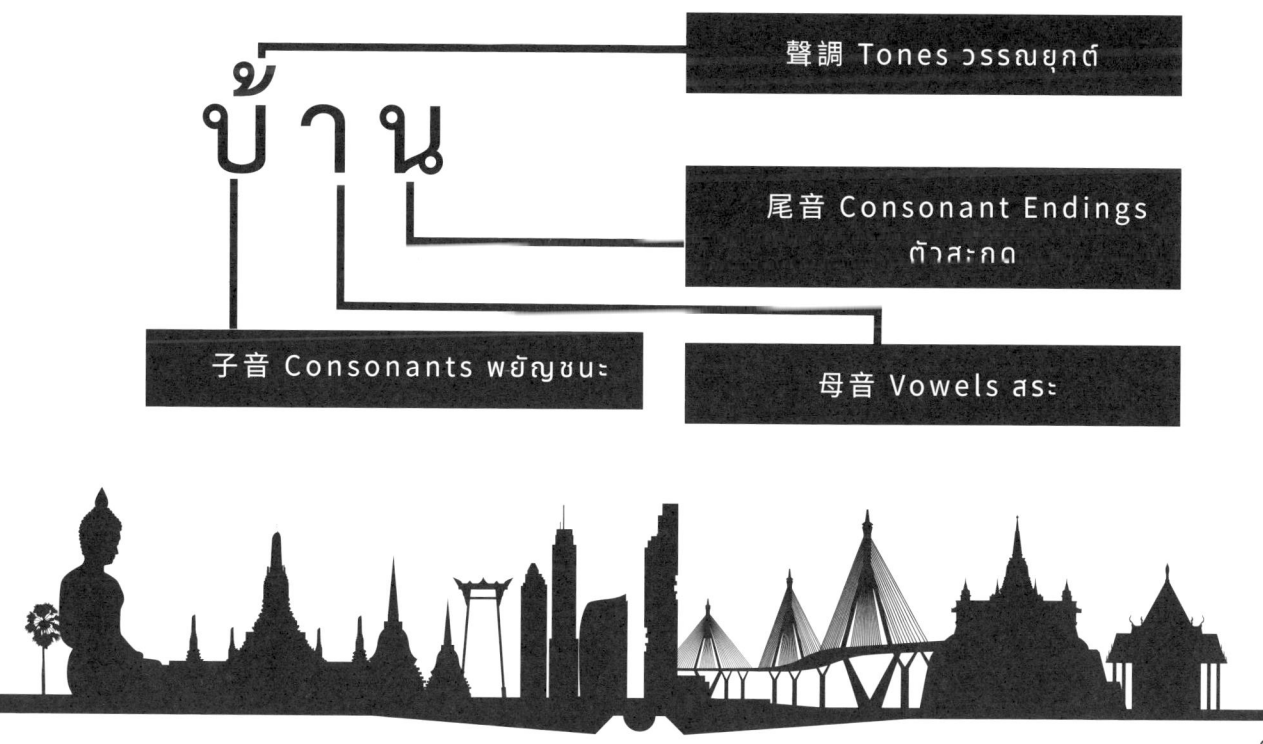

บ้าน

- 聲調 Tones วรรณยุกต์
- 尾音 Consonant Endings ตัวสะกด
- 子音 Consonants พยัญชนะ
- 母音 Vowels สระ

時時泰工作室 | 泰語學習與跨文化交流領導品牌

母音

Vowels สระ

1. 泰語共有 32 個母音，分為單母音、複合母音、特殊母音及獨立母音四大類。單母音有 18 個，包含 9 個短母音和 9 個長母音（編號 1-18）。
2. 複合母音有 6 個，分為 3 個短母音和 3 個長母音（編號 19-24）。
3. 特殊母音與獨立母音各有 4 個（特殊母音編號 25-28，獨立母音編號 29-32）。
4. 「-」為子音的位置，下方以 อ 來做練習。
5. 有標示「#」的母音為簡化母音的一種，即遇到有尾音時，母音會產生變化或簡化。
6. 在母音音標上若顯示「:」，為長母音的標示；若無則為短母音。

1. Thai has 32 vowels, categorized into single vowels, diphthongs, special vowels, and independent vowels.
2. There are 18 single vowels (9 short, 9 long), numbered 1-18. Six diphthongs include 3 short and 3 long vowels, numbered 19-24.
3. There are 4 special vowels (25-28) and 4 independent vowels (29-32).
4. "-" represents the position of the consonant, with อ used for practice below.
5. Vowels marked with "#" are a type of simplified vowel, meaning that when there is a final consonant, the vowel undergoes modification or simplification.
6. If ":" is displayed in the vowel phonetic notation, it indicates a long vowel; if not, it indicates a short vowel.

母音一覽表 Vowels List รายการเสียงสระ

MP3 00-01

#		#		#		#	
1	-ะ [a]	2	-า [a:]	3	-ิ [i]	4	-ี [i:]
5	-ึ [ue]	6	-ือ [ue:]	7	-ุ [u]	8	-ู [u:]
9	เ-ะ [e]	10	เ- [e:]	11	แ-ะ [ae]	12	แ- [ae:]
13	โ-ะ [o]	14	โ- [o:]	15	เ-าะ [or]	16	-อ [or:]
17	เ-อะ [er]	18	เ-อ [er:]	19	เ-ียะ [ia]	20	เ-ีย [i:a]
21	เ-ือะ [uae]	22	เ-ือ [ue:a]	23	-ัวะ [ua]	24	-ัว [u.a]
25	-ำ [am]	26	เ-า [ao]	27	ไ- [ai]	28	ใ- [ai]
29	ฤ [rue]	30	ฤๅ [rue:]	31	ฦ [lue]	32	ฦๅ [lue:]

時時泰工作室 | 泰語學習與跨文化交流領導品牌

子音

Consonants พยัญชนะ

1. 泰語有44個子音，分為中音、高音和低音三類。
2. 中音子音包含9個子音和7個發音，高音子音有11個子音和7個發音，低音子音則有24個子音和14個發音，其中高音子音的ฃ和低音子音的ฅ已不再使用。
3. 不同子音組合會影響聲調，因此熟記每個子音的分類對學習正確發音非常重要。
4. 泰語子音都有「代表單字」，用來區分發音相同但字形和字義不同的字母，學習時需特別注意字首和字尾的發音差異。

1. Thai has 44 consonants, which are divided into three categories: middle, high and low.
2. Middle consonants include 9 consonants and 7 pronunciations, high consonants include 11 consonants and 7 pronunciations, and low consonants include 24 consonants and 14 pronunciations.
3. Among them, ฃ for high consonants and ฅ for low consonants are no longer used.
4. Different combinations of consonants will affect the tone, so it is very important to remember the classification of each consonant to learn correct pronunciation.
5. Thai consonants have "representative words" to distinguish letters with the same pronunciation but different shapes and meanings. When learning, pay special attention to the pronunciation differences between the initials and finals of the words.

中音子音 Middle-pitch consonants อักษรกลาง

MP3 00-02

	子音 Consonants	代表單字 Representative vocabulary	拼音 Pinyin	意思 Meaning	字首 Initial	字尾 Final
1	ก	ไก่	kai2	雞 chicken	k	k
2	จ	จาน	ja:n1	盤子 plate	j	t
3	ด	เด็ก	dek2	小孩 child	t	t
	ฎ	ชฎา	cha4da:1	舞冠 dancer's crown	t	t
4	ต	เต่า	tao2	烏龜 turtle	t	t
	ฏ	ปฏัก	pa2 tak2	刺棍 harpoon	t	t
5	บ	ใบไม้	bai1 mai4	葉子 leaf	b	p
6	ป	ปลา	pla:1	魚 fish	p	p
7	อ	อ่าง	a:ng2	盆子 bowl	o	無 none

時時泰工作室 | 泰語學習與跨文化交流領導品牌

高音子音 High-pitch consonants อักษรสูง

MP3 00-02

	子音 Consonants	代表單字 Representative vocabulary	拼音 Pinyin	意思 Meaning	字首 Initial	字尾 Final
1	ข	ไข่	khai2	蛋 egg	kh	k
	# ฃ	ขวด	khu:at2	瓶子 bottle	kh	無 none
2	ฉ	ฉิ่ง	ching2	小鈸 cymbal	ch	無 none
3	ถ	ถุง	thung5	袋子 bag	th	t
	ฐ	ฐาน	tha:n5	壇 base	th	t
4	ผ	ผึ้ง	phueng3	蜜蜂 bee	ph	無 none
5	ฝ	ฝา	fa:5	蓋子 lid	f	無 none

高音子音 High-pitch consonants อักษรสูง

	子音 Consonants	代表單字 Representative vocabulary	拼音 Pinyin	意思 Meaning	字首 Initial	字尾 Final
6	ศ	ศาลา	sa:5 la:1	涼亭 pavilion	s	t
	ษ	ฤษี	rue:1 si:5	隱修士 hermit	s	t
	ส	เสือ	sue:a5	老虎 tiger	s	t
7	ห	หีบ	ching2	箱子 box	h	無 none

\# ฃ 已不再使用,以 ข 代替。

ฃ is no longer used, replaced by ข

低音子音 MP3 00-13 Low-pitch consonant อักษรต่ำ

	子音 Consonants	代表單字 Representative vocabulary	拼音 Pinyin	意思 Meaning	字首 Initial	字尾 Final
1	# ค	ควาย	kwa:i1	水牛 buffalo	kh	k
1	ฅ	คน	khon1	人 human being	kh	無 none
1	ฆ	ระฆัง	ra4 khang1	鐘 bell	kh	k
2	ช	ช้าง	cha:ng4	大象 elephant	ch	t
2	ฌ	เฌอ	cher:1	大樹 tree	ch	無 none
3	ท	ทหาร	tha4 ha:n5	軍人 soldier	th	t
3	ฑ	มณโฑ	mon1 tho:1	巨人之妻 giant's wife	th	t
3	ฒ	ผู้เฒ่า	phu:3 thao3	老人 older adults	th	t
3	ธ	ธง	thong1	旗 flag	th	t

低音子音 MP3 00-13 Low-pitch consonant อักษรต่ำ

	子音 Consonants	代表單字 Representative vocabulary	拼音 Pinyin	意思 Meaning	字首 Initial	字尾 Final
4	พ	พาน	pha:n1	高腳盤 tray	ph	p
	ภ	สำเภา	sam5 phao1	帆船 sailboat	ph	p
5	ฟ	ฟัน	fan1	牙齒 tooth	f	t
6	ซ	โซ่	so:3	鐵鍊 chain	s	t
7	ฮ	นกฮูก	nok4 hu:k3	貓頭鷹 owl	h	無 none
8	ง	งู	ngu:1	蛇 snake	ng	ng
9	น	หนู	nu:5	老鼠 mouse	n	n
	ณ	เณร	ne:n1	小僧 monk	n	n
10	ม	ม้า	ma:4	馬 horse	m	m

10

時時泰工作室 | 泰語學習與跨文化交流領導品牌

低音子音 MP3 00-13 Low-pitch consonant อักษรต่ำ

	子音 Consonants	代表單字 Representative vocabulary	拼音 Pinyin	意思 Meaning	字首 Initial	字尾 Final
11	ย	ยักษ์	yak4	巨人 giant	y	i
	ญ	หญิง	ying5	女性 women	i	n
12	ร	เรือ	rue:a1	船 boat	r	n
13	ล	ลิง	ling1	猴子 monkey	l	n
	ฬ	จุฬา	ju2 la:1	五角風箏 kite	l	n
14	ว	แหวน	wa:en5	戒指 ring	w	o

ฅ 已不再使用。
ฅ is no longer used.

尾音
Consonant Endings ตัวสะกด

泰語中，位於子音後的子音稱為「尾音」。44 個子音中，只有 35 個可作為尾音，分成 8 組。這 8 組依聲調變化又分為濁尾音和清尾音。

In Thai, consonants after a vowel are called 'final consonants.' Of 44 consonants, 35 can be final consonants, grouped into 8 categories. These are further split into voiced and voiceless final consonants based on tone variation.

	尾音 Consonant endings	發音 Pronunciation	子尾音 Sub-endings
清尾音 Live Consonant endings	ง	[ng]	ง
	ม	[m]	ม
	ย	[i]	ย
	ว	[o]	ว
	น	[n]	น ณ ญ ร ล ฬ
濁尾音 Dead Consonant endings	ก	[k]	ก ข ค ฆ
	บ	[p]	บ ป พ ฟ ภ
	ด	[t]	ท ฑ ฒ ธ ส ศ ษ จ ช ซ ด ฎ ต ฏ ฐ

12

時時泰工作室 | 泰語學習與跨文化交流領導品牌

拼讀規則一：中音子音＋母音
Spelling Rule 1:
Middle-pitch consonants + vowels

กฎการสะกด ๑ อักษรกลาง + สระ

規則 Rule กฎ

中音子音 + 短母音 = 第二聲
中音子音 + 長母音 = 第一聲
中音子音 + 特殊母音 = 第一聲

Middle-pitch consonants + short vowels = second tone
Middle-pitch consonants + long vowels = first tone
Middle-pitch consonants + special vowels = first tone

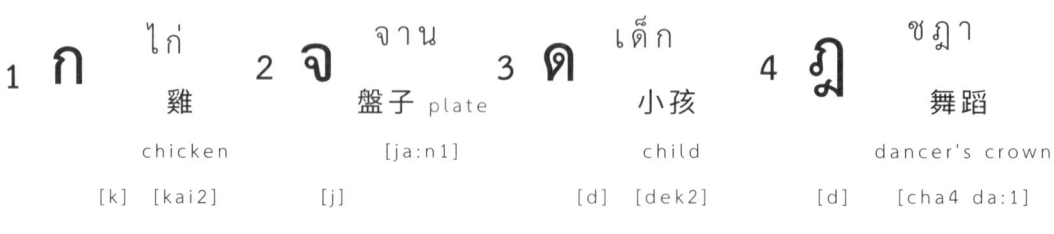

中音子音 Middle-pitch consonants อักษรกลาง MP3 01-01

1 ก ไก่ 雞 chicken [k] [kai2]

2 จ จาน 盤子 plate [ja:n1] [j]

3 ด เด็ก 小孩 child [d] [dek2]

4 ฎ ชฎา 舞蹈 dancer's crown [d] [cha4 da:1]

5 ต เต่า 烏龜 turtle [t] [tao2]

6 ฏ ปฏัก 刺棍 harpoon [t] [pa2 tak2]

7 บ ใบไม้ 葉子 leaf [b] [bai1 mai4]

8 ป ปลา 魚 fish [p] [pla:1]

9 อ อ่าง 盆子 bowl [o] [a:ng2]

13

時時泰工作室｜泰語學習與跨文化交流領導品牌

拼讀表 Spelling table ตารางสะกดคำ

拼讀表 / Spelling table / ตารางสะกด 1

MP3 01-02

	-ะ	-า	-ิ	-ี	-ึ	-ือ	-ุ	-ู	เ-ะ	เ-
ก	กะ ka2	กา ka:1	กิ ki2	กี ki:1	กึ kue2	กือ kue:1	กุ ku2	กู ku:1	เกะ ke2	เก ke:1
จ	จะ ja2	จา ja:1	จิ ji2	จี ji:1	จึ jue2	จือ jue:1	จุ ju2	จู ju:1	เจะ je2	เจ je:1
ด	ดะ da2	ดา da:1	ดิ di2	ดี di:1	ดึ due2	ดือ due:1	ดุ du2	ดู du:1	เดะ de2	เด de:1
ต	ตะ ta2	ตา ta:1	ติ ti2	ตี ti:1	ตึ tue2	ตือ tue:1	ตุ tu2	ตู tu:1	เตะ te2	เต te:1
บ	บะ ba2	บา ba:1	บิ bi2	บี bi:1	บึ bue2	บือ bue:1	บุ bu2	บู bu:1	เบะ be2	เบ be:1
ป	ปะ pa2	ปา pa:1	ปิ pi2	ปี pi:1	ปึ pue2	ปือ pue:1	ปุ pu2	ปู pu:1	เปะ pe2	เป pe:1
อ	อะ a2	อา a:1	อิ i2	อี i:1	อึ ue2	อือ ue:1	อุ u2	อู u:1	เอะ e2	เอ e:1

時時泰工作室｜泰語學習與跨文化交流領導品牌

拼讀表 Spelling table ตารางสะกดคำ

拼讀表 / Spelling table / ตารางสะกด 2

MP3 01-03

	แ-ะ	แ-	โ-ะ	โ-	เ-าะ	-อ	เ-อะ	เ-อ	เ-ียะ
ก	แกะ kae2	แก kae:1	โกะ ko2	โก ko:1	เกาะ kor2	กอ kor:1	เกอะ ker2	เกอ ker:1	เกียะ kia2
จ	แจะ jae2	แจ jae:1	โจะ jo2	โจ jo:1	เจาะ jor2	จอ jor:1	เจอะ jer2	เจอ jer:1	เจียะ jia2
ด	แดะ dae2	แด dae:1	โดะ do2	โด do:1	เดาะ dor2	ดอ dor:1	เดอะ der2	เดอ der:1	เดียะ dia2
ต	แตะ tae2	แต tae:1	โตะ to2	โต to:1	เตาะ tor2	ตอ tor:1	เตอะ ter2	เตอ ter:1	เตียะ tia2
บ	แบะ bae2	แบ bae:1	โบะ bo2	โบ bo:1	เบาะ bor2	บอ bor:1	เบอะ ber2	เบอ ber:1	เบียะ bia2
ป	แปะ pae2	แป pae:1	โปะ po2	โป po:1	เปาะ por2	ปอ por:1	เปอะ per2	เปอ per:1	เปียะ pia2
อ	แอะ ae2	แอ ae:1	โอะ o2	โอ o:1	เอาะ or2	ออ or:1	เออะ er2	เออ er:1	เอียะ ia2

15

時時泰工作室 | 泰語學習與跨文化交流領導品牌

拼讀表 Spelling table ตารางสะกดคำ

拼讀表 / Spelling table / ตารางสะกด 3

MP3 01-04

	เ-ีย	เ-ือะ	เ-ือ	-ัวะ	-ัว	-ำ	ไ-	ใ-	เ-า
ก	เกีย ki:a1	เกือะ kuea2	เกือ kue:a1	กัวะ kua2	กัว ku:a1	กำ kam1	ไก kai1	ใก kai1	เกา kao1
จ	เจีย ji:a1	เจือะ juea2	เจือ jue:a1	จัวะ jua2	จัว ju:a1	จำ jam1	ไจ jai1	ใจ jai1	เจา jao1
ด	เดีย di:a1	เดือะ duea2	เดือ due:a1	ดัวะ dua2	ดัว du:a1	ดำ dam1	ได dai1	ใด dai1	เดา dao1
ต	เตีย ti:a1	เตือะ tuea2	เตือ tue:a1	ตัวะ tua2	ตัว tu:a1	ตำ tam1	ไต tai1	ใต tai1	เตา tao1
บ	เบีย bi:a1	เบือะ buea2	เบือ bue:a1	บัวะ bua2	บัว bu:a1	บำ bam1	ไบ bai1	ใบ bai1	เบา bao1
ป	เปีย pi:a1	เปือะ puea2	เปือ pue:a1	ปัวะ pua2	ปัว pu:a1	ปำ pam1	ไป pai1	ใป pai1	เปา pao1
อ	เอีย i:a1	เอือะ uea2	เอือ ue:a1	อัวะ ua2	อัว u:a1	อำ am1	ไอ ai1	ใอ ai1	เอา ao1

時時泰工作室 | 泰語學習與跨文化交流領導品牌

16

拼讀規則二：高音子音＋母音
Spelling Rule 2:
Hight-pitch consonants + vowels

กฎการสะกด ๒ อักษรสูง + สระ

規則 Rule กฎ

高音子音 + 短母音 = 第二聲
高音子音 + 長母音 = 第五聲
高音子音 + 特殊母音 = 第五聲

High-pitch consonants + short vowels = second tone
High-pitch consonants + long vowels = fifth tone
High-pitch consonants + special vowels = fifth tone

高音子音 High-pitch consonants อักษรสูง   MP3 02-01

1 ข ไข่ 蛋 egg [kh] [khai2]

2 ฃ ขวด 瓶子 bottle [kh] [khu:at2]

3 ฉ ฉิ่ง 小鈸 cymbal [ch] [ching2]

4 ถ ถุง 袋子 bag [th] [thung5]

5 ฐ ฐาน 壇 base [th] [tha:n5]

6 ผ ผึ้ง 蜜蜂 bee [ph] [phueng3]

7 ฝ ฝา 蓋子 lid [f] [fa:5]

8 ศ ศาลา 涼亭 pavilion [s] [sa:5 la:1]

9 ษ ฤๅษี 隱修士 hermit [s] [rue:1 si:5]

10 ส เสือ 老虎 tiger [s] [sue:a5]

11 ห หีบ 箱子 box [h] [hi:p2]

17

時時泰工作室│泰語學習與跨文化交流領導品牌

拼讀表 Spelling table ตารางสะกดคำ

拼讀表 / Spelling table / ตารางสะกด 1

MP3 02-02

	-ะ	-า	-ิ	-ี	-ึ	-ือ	-ุ	-ู	เ-ะ	เ-
ข	ขะ kha2	ขา kha:5	ขิ khi2	ขี khi:5	ขึ khue2	ขือ khue:5	ขุ khu2	ขู khu:5	เขะ khe2	เข khe:5
ฉ	ฉะ cha2	ฉา cha:5	ฉิ chi2	ฉี chi:5	ฉึ chue2	ฉือ chue:5	ฉุ chu2	ฉู chu:5	เฉะ che2	เฉ che:5
ถ	ถะ tha2	ถา tha:5	ถิ thi2	ถี thi:5	ถึ thue2	ถือ thue:5	ถุ thu2	ถู thu:5	เถะ the2	เถ the:5
ผ	ผะ pha2	ผา pha:5	ผิ phi2	ผี phi:5	ผึ phue2	ผือ phue:5	ผุ phu2	ผู phu:5	เผะ phe2	เผ phe:5
ฝ	ฝะ fa2	ฝา fa:5	ฝิ fi2	ฝี fi:5	ฝึ fue2	ฝือ fue:5	ฝุ fu2	ฝู fu:5	เฝะ fe2	เฝ fe:5
ส	สะ sa2	สา sa:5	สิ si2	สี si:5	สึ sue2	สือ sue:5	สุ su2	สู su:5	เสะ se2	เส se:5
ห	หะ ha2	หา ha:5	หิ hi2	หี hi:5	หึ hue2	หือ hue:5	หุ hu2	หู hu:5	เหะ he2	เห he:5

拼讀表 Spelling table ตารางสะกดคำ

拼讀表 / Spelling table / ตารางสะกด 2

MP3 02-03

	แ-ะ	แ-	โ-ะ	โ	เ-าะ	-อ	เ-อะ	เ-อ	เ-ียะ
ข	แขะ khae2	แข khae:5	โขะ kho2	โข kho:5	เขาะ khor2	ขอ khor:5	เขอะ khor:2	เขอ kher:5	เขียะ khia2
ฉ	แฉะ chae2	แฉ chae:5	โฉะ cho2	โฉ cho:5	เฉาะ chor2	ฉอ chor:5	เฉอะ cher:2	เฉอ cher:5	เฉียะ chia2
ถ	แถะ thae2	แถ thae:5	โถะ tho2	โถ tho:5	เถาะ thor2	ถอ thor:5	เถอะ ther:2	เถอ ther:5	เถียะ thia2
ผ	แผะ phae2	แผ phae:5	โผะ pho2	โผ pho:5	เผาะ phor2	ผอ phor:5	เผอะ pher:2	เผอ pher:5	เผียะ phia2
ฝ	แฝะ fae2	แฝ fae:5	โฝะ fo2	โฝ fo:5	เฝาะ for2	ฝอ for:5	เฝอะ fer2	เฝอ fer:5	เฝียะ fia2
ส	แสะ sae2	แส sae:5	โสะ so2	โส so:5	เสาะ sor2	สอ sor:5	เสอะ ser2	เสอ ser:5	เสียะ sia2
ห	แหะ hae2	แห hae:5	โหะ ho2	โห ho:5	เหาะ hor2	หอ hor:5	เหอะ her2	เหอ her:5	เหียะ hia2

拼讀表 Spelling table ตารางสะกดคำ

拼讀表 / Spelling table / ตารางสะกด 3

MP3 02-04

	เ-ีย	เ-ือะ	เ-ือ	-ัวะ	-ัว	-ำ	ไ-	ใ-	เ-า
ข	เขีย khi:a5	เขือะ khuea2	เขือ khue:a5	ขัวะ khua2	ขัว khu:a5	ขำ kham5	ไข khai5	ใข khai5	เขา khao5
ฉ	เฉีย chi:a5	เฉือะ chuea2	เฉือ chue:a5	ฉัวะ chua2	ฉัว chu:a5	ฉำ cham5	ไฉ chai5	ใฉ chai5	เฉา chao5
ถ	เถีย thi:a5	เถือะ thuea2	เถือ thue:a5	ถัวะ thua2	ถัว thu:a5	ถำ tham5	ไถ thai5	ใถ thai5	เถา thao5
ผ	เผีย phi:a5	เผือะ phuea2	เผือ phue:a5	ผัวะ phua2	ผัว phu:a5	ผำ pham5	ไผ phai5	ใผ phai5	เผา phao5
ฝ	เฝีย fi:a5	เฝือะ fuea2	เฝือ fue:a5	ฝัวะ fua2	ฝัว fu:a5	ฝำ fam5	ไฝ fai5	ใฝ fai5	เฝา fao5
ส	เสีย si:a5	เสือะ suea2	เสือ sue:a5	สัวะ sua2	สัว su:a5	สำ sam5	ไส sai5	ใส sai5	เสา sao5
ห	เหีย hi:a5	เหือะ huea2	เหือ hue:a5	หัวะ hua2	หัว hu:a5	หำ ham5	ไห hai5	ให hai5	เหา hao5

時時泰工作室 | 泰語學習與跨文化交流領導品牌

拼讀規則三：低音子音＋母音
Spelling Rule 3:
Low-pitch consonants + vowels

กฎการสะกด ๒ อักษรต่ำ + สระ

規則 Rule กฎ

低音子音 + 短母音 = 第四聲
低音子音 + 長母音 = 第一聲
低音子音 + 特殊母音 = 第一聲

Low-pitch consonants + short vowels = fourth tone
Low-pitch consonants + long vowels = first tone
Low-pitch consonants + special vowels = first tone

低音子音 Low-pitch consonants อักษรต่ำ

MP3 03-01

1 **ค** ควาย 水牛 buffalo [kh] [kwa:i1]

2 **ค** คน 人 human being [kh] [khon1]

3 **ฆ** ระฆัง 大鐘 bell [kh] [ra4 khang1]

4 **ช** ช้าง 大象 elephant [ch] [cha:ng4]

5 **ฌ** เฌอ 大樹 tree [ch] [cher:1]

6 **ท** ทหาร 軍人 soldier [th] [tha4 ha:n5]

7 **ฑ** มณโฑ 巨人之妻 giant's wife [th] [mon1 tho:1]

8 **ฒ** ผู้เฒ่า 老人 older adults [th] [phu:3 thao3]

1 ธ ธง 旗子 flag [th] [thong1]	2 พ พาน 高腳盤 tray [ph] [pha:n1]	3 ภ สำเภา 帆船 sailboat [ph] [sam5 phao1]	4 ฟ ฟัน 牙齒 tooth [f] [fan1]
1 ซ โซ่ 鐵鍊 chain [s] [so:3]	2 ฮ นกฮูก 貓頭鷹 owl [h] [nok4 hu:k3]	3 ง งู 蛇 snake [ng] [ngu:1]	4 น หนู 老鼠 mouse [n] [nu:5]
1 ณ เณร 小僧 monk [n] [ne:n1]	2 ม ม้า 馬 horse [m] [ma:4]	3 ย ยักษ์ 巨人 giant [y] [yak4]	4 ญ หญิง 女性 women [y] [ying5]
1 ร เรือ 船 boat [r] [rue:a1]	2 ล ลิง 猴子 monkey [l] [ling1]	3 ฬ จุฬา 五角風箏 kite [l] [ju2 la:1]	4 ว แหวน 戒指 ring [w] [wae:n5]

時時泰工作室 | 泰語學習與跨文化交流領導品牌

拼讀表 Spelling table ตารางสะกดคำ

拼讀表 / Spelling table / ตารางสะกด 1

MP3 03-02

	-ะ	-า	-ิ	-ี	-ื	-อ	-ุ	-ู	เ-ะ	เ-
ค	คะ kha4	คา kha:1	คิ khi4	คี khi:1	คื khue4	คือ khue:1	คุ khu4	คู khu:1	เคะ khe4	เค khe:1
ช	ชะ cha4	ชา cha:1	ชิ chi4	ชี chi:1	ชื chue4	ชือ chue:1	ชุ chu4	ชู chu:1	เชะ che4	เช che:1
ท	ทะ tha4	ทา tha:1	ทิ thi4	ที thi:1	ทื thue4	ทือ thue:1	ทุ thu4	ทู thu:1	เทะ the4	เท the:1
พ	พะ pha4	พา pha:1	พิ phi4	พี phi:1	พื phue4	พือ phue:1	พุ phu4	พู phu:1	เพะ phe4	เพ phe:1
ฟ	ฟะ fa4	ฟา fa:1	ฟิ fi4	ฟี fi:1	ฟื fue4	ฟือ fue:1	ฟุ fu4	ฟู fu:1	เฟะ fe4	เฟ fe:1
ซ	ซะ sa4	ซา sa:1	ซิ si4	ซี si:1	ซื sue4	ซือ sue:1	ซุ su4	ซู su:1	เซะ se4	เซ se:1
ฮ	ฮะ ha4	ฮา ha:1	ฮิ hi4	ฮี hi:1	ฮื hue4	ฮือ hue:1	ฮุ hu4	ฮู hu:1	เฮะ he4	เฮ he:1

時時泰工作室 | 泰語學習與跨文化交流領導品牌

拼讀表 Spelling table ตารางสะกดคำ

拼讀表 / Spelling table / ตารางสะกด 2

MP3 03-03

	แ-ะ	แ-	โ-ะ	โ	เ-าะ	-อ	เ-อะ	เ-อ	เ-ียะ
ค	แคะ khae4	แค khae:1	โคะ kho4	โค kho:1	เคาะ khor4	คอ khor:1	เคอะ kher4	เคอ kher:1	เคียะ kia4
ช	แชะ chae4	แช chae:1	โชะ cho4	โช cho:1	เชาะ chor4	ชอ chor:1	เชอะ cher4	เชอ cher:1	เชียะ chia4
ท	แทะ thae4	แท thae:1	โทะ tho4	โท tho:1	เทาะ thor4	ทอ thor:1	เทอะ ther4	เทอ ther:1	เทียะ thia4
พ	แพะ phae4	แพ phae:1	โพะ pho4	โพ pho:1	เพาะ phor4	พอ phor:1	เพอะ pher4	เพอ pher:1	เพียะ phia4
ฟ	แฟะ fae4	แฟ fae:1	โฟะ fo4	โฟ fo:1	เฟาะ for4	ฟอ for:1	เฟอะ fer4	เฟอ fer:1	เฟียะ fia4
ซ	แซะ sae4	แซ sae:1	โซะ so4	โซ so:1	เซาะ sor4	ซอ sor:1	เซอะ ser4	เซอ ser:1	เซียะ sia4
ฮ	แฮะ hae4	แฮ hae:1	โฮะ ho4	โฮ ho:1	เฮาะ hor4	ฮอ hor:1	เฮอะ her4	เฮอ her:1	เฮียะ hia4

時時泰工作室 | 泰語學習與跨文化交流領導品牌

拼讀表 Spelling table ตารางสะกดคำ

拼讀表 / Spelling table / ตารางสะกด 3

MP3 03-04

	เ-ีย	เ-ือะ	เ-ือ	-ัวะ	-ัว	-ำ	ไ-	ใ-	เ-า
ค	เคีย khi:a1	เคือะ khuea4	เคือ khue:a1	ควะ khua4	คัว khu:a1	คำ kham1	ไค khai1	ใค khai1	เคา khao1
ช	เชีย chi:a1	เชือะ chuea4	เชือ chue:a1	ชัวะ chua4	ชัว chu:a1	ชำ cham1	ไช chai1	ใช chai1	เชา chao1
ท	เทีย thi:a1	เทือะ thuea4	เทือ thue:a1	ทัวะ thua4	ทัว thu:a1	ทำ tham1	ไท thai1	ใท thai1	เทา thao1
พ	เพีย phi:a1	เพือะ phuea4	เพือ phue:a1	พัวะ phua4	พัว phu:a1	พำ pham1	ไพ phai1	ใพ phai1	เพา phao1
ฟ	เฟีย fi:a1	เฟือะ fuea4	เฟือ fue:a1	ฟัวะ fua4	ฟัว fu:a1	ฟำ fam1	ไฟ fai1	ใฟ fai1	เฟา fao1
ซ	เซีย si:a1	เซือะ suea4	เซือ sue:a1	ซัวะ sua4	ซัว su:a1	ซำ sam1	ไซ sai1	ใซ sai1	เซา sao1
ฮ	เฮีย hi:a1	เฮือะ huea4	เฮือ hue:a1	ฮัวะ hua4	ฮัว hu:a1	ฮำ ham1	ไฮ hai1	ใฮ hai1	เฮา hao1

時時泰工作室｜泰語學習與跨文化交流領導品牌

拼讀表 Spelling table ตารางสะกดคำ

拼讀表 / Spelling table / ตารางสะกด 1

MP3 03-05

	-ะ	-า	-ิ	-ี	-ึ	-ือ	-ุ	-ู	เ-ะ	เ-
ง	งะ nga4	งา nga:1	งิ ngi4	งี ngi:1	งึ ngue4	งือ ngue:1	งุ ngu4	งู ngu:1	เงะ nge4	เง nge:1
น	นะ na4	นา na:1	นิ ni4	นี ni:1	นึ nue4	นือ nue:1	นุ nu4	นู nu:1	เนะ ne4	เน ne:1
ม	มะ ma4	มา ma:1	มิ mi4	มี mi:1	มึ mue4	มือ mue:1	มุ mu4	มู mu:1	เมะ me4	เม me:1
ย	ยะ ya4	ยา ya:1	ยิ yi4	ยี yi:1	ยึ yue4	ยือ yue:1	ยุ yu4	ยู yu:1	เยะ ye4	เย ye:1
ร	ระ ra4	รา ra:1	ริ ri4	รี ri:1	รึ rue4	รือ rue:1	รุ ru4	รู ru:1	เระ re4	เร re:1
ล	ละ la4	ลา la:1	ลิ li4	ลี li:1	ลึ lue4	ลือ lue:1	ลุ lu4	ลู lu:1	เละ le4	เล le:1
ว	วะ wa4	วา wa:1	วิ wi4	วี wi:1	วึ wue4	วือ wue:1	วุ wu4	วู wu:1	เวะ we4	เว we:1

時時泰工作室 | 泰語學習與跨文化交流領導品牌

拼讀表 Spelling table ตารางสะกดคำ

拼讀表 / Spelling table / ตารางสะกด 2

MP3 03-06

	แ-ะ	แ-	โ-ะ	โ	เ-าะ	-อ	เ-อะ	เ-อ	เ-ียะ
ง	แงะ ngae4	แง nguae:1	โงะ ngo4	โง ngo:1	เงาะ ngor4	งอ ngor:1	เงอะ nger:4	เงอ nger:1	เงียะ ngia4
น	แนะ nae4	แน nae:1	โนะ no4	โน no:1	เนาะ nor4	นอ nor:1	เนอะ ner:4	เนอ ner:1	เนียะ nia4
ม	แมะ mae4	แม mae:1	โมะ mo4	โม mo:1	เมาะ mor4	มอ mor:1	เมอะ mer:4	เมอ mer:1	เมียะ mia4
ย	แยะ yae4	แย yuae:1	โยะ yo4	โย yo:1	เยาะ yor4	ยอ yor:1	เยอะ yer:4	เยอ yer:1	เยียะ yia4
ร	แระ rae4	แร rae:1	โระ ro4	โร ro:1	เราะ ror4	รอ ror:1	เรอะ rer:4	เรอ rer:1	เรียะ ria4
ล	และ lae4	แล lae:1	โละ lo4	โล lo:1	เลาะ lor4	ลอ lor:1	เลอะ ler:4	เลอ ler:1	เลียะ lia4
ว	แวะ wae4	แว wuae:1	โวะ wo4	โว wo:1	เวาะ wor4	วอ wor:1	เวอะ wer:4	เวอ wer:1	เวียะ wia4

時時泰工作室 | 泰語學習與跨文化交流領導品牌

拼讀表 Spelling table ตารางสะกดคำ

拼讀表 / Spelling table / ตารางสะกด 3

MP3 03-07

	เ-ีย	เ-ือะ	เ-ือ	-ัวะ	-ัว	-ำ	ไ-	ใ-	เ-า
ง	เงีย ngi:a1	เงือะ nguea4	เงือ ngue:a1	งัวะ ngua4	งัว ngu:a1	งำ ngam1	ไง ngai1	ใง ngai1	เงา ngao1
น	เนีย ni:a1	เนือะ nuea4	เนือ nue:a1	นัวะ nua4	นัว nu:a1	นำ nam1	ไน nai1	ใน nai1	เนา nao1
ม	เมีย mi:a1	เมือะ muea4	เมือ mue:a1	มัวะ mua4	มัว mu:a1	มำ mam1	ไม mai1	ใม mai1	เมา mao1
ย	เยีย yi:a1	เยือะ yuea4	เยือ yue:a1	ยัวะ yua4	ยัว yu:a1	ยำ yam1	ไย yai1	ใย yai1	เยา yao1
ร	เรีย ri:a1	เรือะ ruea4	เรือ rue:a1	รัวะ rua4	รัว ru:a1	รำ ram1	ไร rai1	ใร rai1	เรา rao1
ล	เลีย li:a1	เลือะ luea4	เลือ lue:a1	ลัวะ lua4	ลัว lu:a1	ลำ lam1	ไล lai1	ใล lai1	เลา lao1
ว	เวีย wi:a1	เวือะ wuea4	เวือ wue:a1	วัวะ wua4	วัว wu:a1	วำ wam1	ไว wai1	ใว wai1	เวา wao1

時時泰工作室｜泰語學習與跨文化交流領導品牌

拼讀規則四：簡化母音
Spelling Rule 4 : Simplified Vowels
กฎการสะกด ๔ สระเปลี่ยนรูป

規則 Rule กฎ

當母音加上「尾音」時，母音會被簡化，泰語中共有七組簡化母音。
其中有 ◌ั 、 ◌็ 兩個新符號得產生。

When the "consonant endings" is added to the vowel, the vowel will be simplified. In the Thai system there are seven groups of simplified vowels. Among them, they are two new symbols and ◌ั and ◌็.

MP3 04-01

母音 Vowel	發音 Pronunciation	簡化母音 Simplified Vowels	例子 Example	拼音 Pinyin	中文 Chinese	英文 English
1.-ะ	[a]	◌ั	ว+ะ+น = วัน	wan1	天	day
2.เ-ะ	[e]	เ◌็	เหะ+น = เห็น	hen5	看見	see
3.แ-ะ	[ae]	แ◌็	แชะ+ต = แช็ต	chae:t4	聊天	chat
4.โ-ะ	[o]	-	โบะ+น = บน	bon1	在上面	on
5.เ-าะ	[or]	◌็-อ	เราะ+ก = ร็อก	rork4	搖滾	rock
6.เ-อ	[er:]	เ-ิ	เกอ+น = เกิน	ker:n1	超過	exceed
7.-ัว	[u:a]	-ว-	สัว+น = สวน	suan5	花園	garden

29

拼讀規則五：聲調符號
Spelling Rule 5 : Tone
กฎการสะกด ๗ วรรณยุกต์

泰語有五種聲調，每個聲調都有專屬符號，但每個音節無論有無符號都帶有聲調。沒有符號的聲調稱為「基本聲調(พื้นเสียง)」，但不一定是第一聲調（以紅字標示）。本書中，聲調以數字1至5表示，分別對應第一至第五聲調。

Thai has five tones, each represented by a specific symbol. However, every syllable carries a tone, regardless of whether it has a symbol or not. Tones without symbols are referred to as "basic tones (พื้นเสียง)," but they are not necessarily the first tone (highlighted in red). In this book, tones are represented by numbers 1 to 5, corresponding to the first to fifth tones, respectively.

MP3 05-01

聲調符號示意圖 Symbol Illustration ภาพประกอบสัญลักษณ์

第一聲 First Tone	第二聲 Second Tone	第三聲 Third Tone	第四聲 Fourth Tone	第五聲 Fifth Tone
無聲調符號 no tone symbol	่	้	๊	๋
→	↘↗	↘	↗↘↗	↗
กา ka : 1	ก่า ka : 2	ก้า ka : 3	ก๊า ka : 4	ก๋า ka : 5

30

時時泰工作室 | 泰語學習與跨文化交流領導品牌

中音子音拼讀規則
Rules for the pronunciation of middle-pitch consonants
กฎสำหรับการออกเสียงพยัญชนะเสียงกลาง

1. 中音子音配短母音時，多數讀第二聲（無聲調符號），僅少數單字帶有聲調符號。
2. 中音子音配長母音時，通常讀第一聲（無聲調符號），若帶聲調符號則可發出五種聲調。

1. When incorporating the short vowel, the second tone is primarily pronounced (without a tone symbol), with only a limited number of words featuring tone symbols.
2. For middle-pitch consonants paired with the long vowel, the first tone (without a tone symbol) is pronounced, and adding a tone symbol allows for the possibility of five distinct tones.

MP3 05-02

範例 Example	第一聲 First Tone	第二聲 Second Tone	第三聲 Third Tone	第四聲 Fourth Tone	第五聲 Fifth Tone
中音子音＋短母音 middle-pitch consonants+ short vowel		กะ ka 2	ก่ะ ka 3	ก้ะ ka 4	ก๊ะ ka 5
中音子音＋長母音 middle-pitch consonants+ long vowel	กา ka:1	ก่า ka:2	ก้า ka:3	ก๊า ka:4	ก๋า ka:5
中音子音＋特殊母音 middle-pitch consonants+ special vowel	ไก kai 1	ไก่ kai 2	ไก้ kai 3	ไก๊ kai 4	ไก๋ kai 5

高音子音拼讀規則
Rules for the pronunciation of middle-pitch consonants
กฎสำหรับการออกเสียงพยัญชนะเสียงสูง

1. 高音子音配短母音時，只能發第二聲，如下表所示。
2. 高音子音配長母音時，可發第二聲、第三聲及第五聲。

1. When high-pitched consonants and short vowels are included, only the second tones can be represented.
2. When high-pitched consonants are paired with long vowels, the second, third, and fifth tones are articulated.

MP3 05-03

範例 Example	第二聲 Second Tone	第三聲 Third Tone	第五聲 Fifth Tone
高音子音＋短母音 high-pitch consonants+ short vowel	ขะ kha 2	ข้ะ kha 3	
高音子音＋長母音 high-pitch consonants+ long vowel	ข่า kha:2	ข้า kha:3	ขา kha:5
高音子音＋特殊母音 high-pitch consonants+ special vowel	เข่า khao 2	เข้า khao 3	เขา khao 5

低音子音拼讀規則
Rules for the pronunciation of low-pitch consonants
กฎสำหรับการออกเสียงพยัญชนะเสียงต่ำ

1. 低音子音加短母音時，只能拼出第四聲，僅少數單字可拼出第三聲。
2. 低音子音加長母音時，發第一聲、第三聲和第四聲。

1. When the low-pitch consonants and short vowels are added, only the fourth tones can be spelled out.
2. When the low-pitch consonants with the long vowel, the first, third and fourth tones are pronounced.

MP3 05-04

範例 Example	第一聲 First Tone	第三聲 Third Tone	第四聲 Fourth Tone
低音子音＋短母音 low-pitch consonants+ short vowel		ค่ะ kha 3	คะ kha 4
低音子音＋長母音 low-pitch consonants+ long vowel	คา kha:1	ค่า kha:3	ค้า kha:4
低音子音＋特殊母音 low-pitch consonants+ special vowel	คำ kham 1	ค่ำ kham 3	ค้ำ kham 4

泰語規則六：前引字
Thai Rule 6 : Leading consonant
กฎการสะกด ๘ อักษรนำ

泰語的音節由母音、中音子音、高音子音和低音子音組成。在聲調方面，中音子音可發出五個聲調，而高音子音和低音子音雖無法單獨發出五個聲調，但透過對應的讀音組合，仍能表達五個聲調。以下是具體的聲調對應表。

MP3 06-01

Thai is composed of vowels along with middle-pitch, high-pitch, and low-pitch consonants. Regarding tones, only middle-pitch consonants have the ability to generate five distinct tones. While high-pitch and low-pitch consonants cannot independently produce these five tones, they can be paired with corresponding pronunciations to create the same tonal variety. Below is a table that illustrates this concept:

範例 Example	第一聲 First Tone	第二聲 Second Tone	第三聲 Third Tone	第四聲 Fourth Tone	第五聲 Fifth Tone
中音子音 Middle-pitch consonants	กา ka : 1	ก่า ka : 2	ก้า ka : 3	ก๊า ka : 4	ก๋า ka : 5
高音子音 High-pitch consonants		ข่า kha : 2	ข้า kha : 3		ขา kha : 5
低音子音 Low-pitch consonants	คา kha : 1		ค่า kha : 3	ค้า kha : 4	

部分低音子音無法由高音子音找到對應讀音，例如：ง、ญ、ณ、ย、ม、ร、ล、ว、ฤ，需依靠「前引字」協助，才能正確表達聲調。

Certain low-pitch consonants are unable to independently generate their corresponding pronunciations with high-pitch consonants. Examples include ง, ญ, ณ, ย, ม, ร, ล, and ว. These consonants need a "leading consonant" to effectively produce tones that would otherwise be unexpressed.

34

前引字通常位於音節前方，當子音由前引字引導時，其發音依前引字的字母發音規則進行。前引字可分為不發音前引字與發音前引字。

The Role of Leading Consonants in Syllables

The leading consonant typically appears at the beginning of a syllable. When a consonant is influenced by the leading consonant, its pronunciation adheres to the rules set by that consonant. Leading consonants can be categorized into two types: silent leading consonants and those that are pronounced.

不發音前引字 Silent leading consonant เงียบอักษรนำ

ห 前引字母在泰語中常見，雖然不發音但會影響聲調。

It is more common for ห to serve as the leading letters. While it is not pronounced, it does influence the tone.

MP3 06-02

泰文 Thai	發音 Pronounce	拼音 Pinyin	中文 Chinese	英文 English
หมา	ห-มา	ma:5	狗	(n.) dog
หมู่	ห-มู่	mu:2	群組	(n.) group
หงาย	ห-งาย	ngai:5	仰面	(v.) face up
หยิบ	ห-ยิบ	yip2	拿起	(v.) pick up
หวาน	ห-วาน	wan5	甜	(adj.) sweet

อ   泰語中目前僅有四個單字以引字母開頭。

When the letters "อ" appear at the beginning, there are only four words in Thai:

MP3 06-03

泰文 Thai	發音 Pronounce	拼音 Pinyin	中文 Chinese	英文 English
อย่า	อย่า	ya:2	不要、別…	don't
อยู่	อยู่	yu:2	在、居住、生活	is (located at); stay; live
อย่าง	อย่าง	ya:ng2	樣式、種類	variety; style; type
อยาก	อยาก	ya:k2	想要、渴望	to want; to desire; to crave for

＊ห 自身無發音，依照中音子音的發音規則進行發聲。

It does not produce sound on its own but follows the pronunciation rules of the middle consonants.

練習 Practice แบบฝึกหัด

請嘗試朗讀以下句子。
Try reading the following sentence aloud.

MP3 06-04

泰文 Thai	發音 Pronounce	拼音 Pinyin
1. อย่า กังวล ya:2 kang1 won1	別擔心	Don't worry
2. ทำ งาน อย่าง ดี tham1 nga:n1 ya:ng2 di:1	很好地工作	work well
3. อยู่ ดี กิน ดี yu:2 di:1 kin1 di:1	豐衣足食	live well
4. อยู่ ด้วย กัน yu2 du:a3 kan1	住在一起	live together
5. อยาก กิน ข้าว yak2 kin1 khao3	想吃飯	want to eat rice
6. ฉัน อยาก อยู่ เมืองไทย chan5 ya:k2 yu2 mue:ang1 thai1	我想待在泰國	I want to stay in Thailand
7. เขา ทำ งาน อย่าง รวด เร็ว khao5 tham1 nga:n1 yang2 ru:at3 reo1	他工作很快	He works quickly

時時泰工作室 | 泰語學習與跨文化交流領導品牌

發音前引字 Pronunciate leading consonant อักษรนำ

當高音子音 ข、ฉ、ถ、ผ、ฝ、ศ、ส、ห 作為前引字時,需在其後添加短母音 ะ (a),且被前引的部分需依高音子音的發音規則進行發音。

If a high-pitch consonant such as ข, ฉ, ถ, ผ, ฝ, ศ, ส, or ห is used as the leading consonant, it is essential to add the short vowel ะ (a). The pronunciation should adhere to the guidelines for high-pitch consonants. MP3 06-05

泰文 Thai	發音 Pronounce	拼音 Pinyin	中文 Chinese	英文 English
ฉลาด	ฉะ-ลาด	cha2 la:t2	聰明	smart
เสมอ	สะ-หมอ	sa2 mer:5	總是	always

由中音子音 ก、จ、ฎ、ฏ、ฐ、ฒ、บ、ป、อ 作為前引字時,需加上短母音 ะ (a),被前引的部分則依照中音子音的發音規則進行發音。

If a middle-pitch consonant—ก, จ, ฎ, ฏ, ฐ, ฒ, บ, ป, or อ—is utilized as the initial consonant, the short vowel ะ (a) must be included. The pronunciation should adhere to the established rules governing the middle-pitch consonants.

泰文 Thai	發音 Pronounce	拼音 Pinyin	中文 Chinese	英文 English
ตลอด	ตะ-หลอด	ld2 lur:l2	始終、一直	throughout

基礎泰文拼讀練習

Basic Thai Phonics Practice

中音子音與母音：拼讀練習 MP3 07-01

說明：
請大聲朗讀以下單字與詞組，注意中音子音與母音的發音。
建議每題反覆練習3次。

Middle-pitch consonants and Vowels: Phonics Practice
Instructions:
Please read the following words and phrases aloud, paying attention to the pronunciation of consonants and vowels.
It is recommended to practice each item three times.

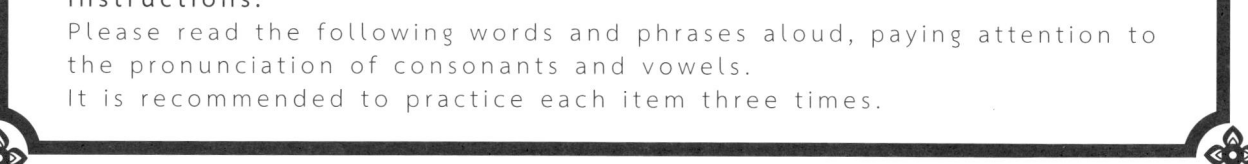

	書寫 Writing	意思 Meaning
1. บิดา		
2. ปา		
3. ปะ		
4. จะ		
5. ดู		
6. ดุ		
7. ตี		
8. จำ		
9. ตา		
10. เตะ		

40

時時泰工作室 | 泰語學習與跨文化交流領導品牌

中音子音與母音：拼讀練習

說明：
請大聲朗讀以下單字與詞組，注意中音子音與母音的發音。
建議每題反覆練習3次。

Middle-pitch consonants and Vowels: Phonics Practice
Instructions:
Please read the following words and phrases aloud, paying attention to the pronunciation of consonants and vowels.
It is recommended to practice each item three times.

	書寫 Writing	意思 Meaning
11. ปู	_____	_____
12. ปี	_____	_____
13. แกะ	_____	_____
14. อาตีปู	_____	_____
15. เจอ	_____	_____
16. เบา	_____	_____
17. ตะ	_____	_____
18. อา	_____	_____
19. เกาะ	_____	_____
20. เอา	_____	_____

中音子音與母音：選擇題練習

請從以下選項中選擇正確的泰文單字或發音

Multiple Choice Practice
Please choose the correct Thai word or pronunciation from the options below.

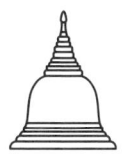

1. 表示「父親」的單字是
The word for "Father" is
 a) บิดา   b) ตา   c) อา   d) ปา

2. 表示「扔」的單字是
The word for "Throw" is
 a) ปา   b) ปะ   c) ปู   d) ปี

3. 「จะ」的正確發音是
The correct pronunciation of "จะ" is
 a) ja2   b) cha2   c) ya2   d) ka2

4. 表示「看」的單字是
The word for "Look" is
 a) ดู   b) ดุ   c) ตี   d) เจอ

5. 「ตา」的意思是
The meaning of "ตา" is
 a) 眼睛 eye   b) 鼻子 nose   c) 耳朵 ear   d) 嘴巴 mouth

6. 「ปู」的正確發音是
The correct pronunciation of "ปู" is
 a) pu:1   b) bu:1   c) tu:1   d) ku:1

7. 表示「年」的單字是
The word for "Year" is
 a) ปี   b) ปู   c) ปะ   d) ปิด

中音子音與母音：選擇題練習

請從以下選項中選擇正確的泰文單字或發音
Multiple Choice Practice
Please choose the correct Thai word or pronunciation from the options below.

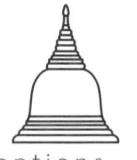

8.「เตะ」的意思是
The word for "เตะ" is
 a) 跑 run   b) 踢 kick   c) 跳 jump   d) 走 walk

9.「จำ」的正確發音是
The correct pronunciation of "จำ" is
 a) jam1   b) cham1   c) tam1   d) kam 1

10. 表示「羊」的單字是
The meaning of "Sheep" is
 a) แกะ   b) เกาะ   c) เจอ   d) เบา

11.「เอา」的意思是
The word for "เอา" is
 a) 拿 to take   b) 給 to give   c) 放 to put   d) 丟 to throw

12.「ดุ」的正確發音是
The correct pronunciation of "ดุ" is
 a) du:2   b) tu2   c) du2   d) chu:2

13. 表示「島」的單字是
The word for "Island" is
 a) เกาะ   b) แกะ   c) ตะ   d) อา

14.「เบา」的意思是
The word for "เบา" is
 a) 重 heavy   b) 輕 light   c) 大 big   d) 小 small

15.「ปิด」的正確發音是
The correct pronunciation of "ปิด" is
 a) pit2   b) bit2   c) tit2   d) jit2

高音子音與母音：拼讀練習

MP3 08-01

說明：
請大聲朗讀以下單字與詞組，注意高音子音與母音的發音。
建議每題反覆練習3次。

High-pitch Consonants and Vowels: Phonics Practice
Instructions:
Please read the following words and phrases aloud, paying attention to the pronunciation of consonants and vowels.
It is recommended to practice each item three times.

	書寫 Writing	意思 Meaning
1. ขา		
2. ถือ		
3. ฐู		
4. ผา		
5. เสียใจ		
6. เสือ		
7. เขา		
8. สาขา		
9. เสา		
10. สา		

高音子音與母音：拼讀練習

說明：
請大聲朗讀以下單字與詞組，注意高音子音與母音的發音。
建議每題反覆練習3次。

High-pitch Consonants and Vowels: Phonics Practice
Instructions:
Please read the following words and phrases aloud, paying attention to the pronunciation of consonants and vowels.
It is recommended to practice each item three times.

	書寫 Writing	意思 Meaning
11. โส		
12. เฉา		
13. สี		
14. ใส		
15. หาผี		
16. หู		
17. หอ		
18. ชี		
19. โผ		
20. แฉ		

高音子音與母音：選擇題練習

請從以下選項中選擇正確的泰文單字或發音

Multiple Choice Practice
Please select the correct Thai word or pronunciation from the options below.

1.表示「腿」的單字
The word for "Leg" is
 a) ขา　　　　b) สา　　　　c) หา　　　　d) เสา

2.表示「擦」的單字是
The word for "Wipe" is
 a) ถู　　　　b) ถือ　　　　c) สู　　　　d) หู

3.「ผา」的正確發音是
The correct pronunciation of "ผา" is
 a) pha:5　　　b) pa:5　　　c) pho:5　　　d) po:5

4.表示「老虎」的單字是
The word for "Tiger" is
 a) เสือ　　　　b) เสา　　　　c) สี　　　　d) ใส

5.「เสียใจ」的意思是
The meaning of "เสียใจ" is
 a) 開心 happy　b) 難過 sad　c) 生氣 hungry　d) 害怕 scared

6.「เขา」的正確發音是
The correct pronunciation of "เขา" is
 a) khao5　　　b) kao5　　　c) hao5　　　　d) sao5

7.表示「透明」的單字是
The word for "Transparent" is
 a) ใส　　　　b) สี　　　　c) สาย　　　　d) เสีย

高音子音與母音：選擇題練習

請從以下選項中選擇正確的泰文單字或發音

Multiple Choice Practice

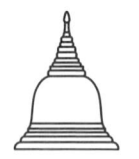

Please select the correct Thai word or pronunciation from the options below.

8. 「หู」的意思是
The correct pronunciation of "หู" is
 a) 鼻子 nose   b) 耳朵 ears   c) 嘴巴 mouth   d) 眼睛 eyes

9. 「สาขา」正確發音是
The correct pronunciation of "สาขา" is
 a) sa:5kha:5   b) sai:5kha:5   c) sa:5ha:5   d) sa:5ka:5

10. 表示「乾枯」的單字是
The word for "Withered" is
 a) เฉา   b) ฉาย   c) ชา   d) สู

11. 「ผี」的意思是
The word for "ผี" is
 a) 鬼 ghost   b) 人 person   c) 動物 animal   d) 植物 plant

12. 「ถู」的正確發音是
The correct pronunciation of "ฉาย" is
 a) thu:5   b) su:5   c) phu:5   d) ju:5

13. 表示「找」的單字是
The word for "Sell" is
 a) หา   b) หอ   c) สา   d) ขี

14. 「หอ」的意思是
The word for "หอ" is
 a) 房子 house   b) 塔 tower   c) 學校 school   d) 市場 market

15. 「สี」的正確發音是
The correct pronunciation of "สี" is
 a) si 5   b) sai:5   c) si:5   d) shi:5

低音子音與母音：拼讀練習 MP3 09-01

說明：
請大聲朗讀以下單字與詞組，注意低音子音與母音的發音。
建議每題反覆練習3次。

Low-pitch Consonants and Vowels: Phonics Practice
Instructions:
Please read the following words and phrases aloud, paying attention to the pronunciation of consonants and vowels.
It is recommended to practice each item three times.

	書寫 Writing	意思 Meaning
1. คำ		
2. ยา		
3. มา		
4. คือ		
5. เงาะ		
6. ใย		
7. แพะ		
8. เท		
9. พา		
10. เงา		

低音子音與母音：拼讀練習

說明：
請大聲朗讀以下單字與詞組，注意低音子音與母音的發音。
建議每題反覆練習3次。

Low-pitch Consonants and Vowels: Phonics Practice
Instructions:
Please read the following words and phrases aloud, paying attention to the pronunciation of consonants and vowels.
It is recommended to practice each item three times.

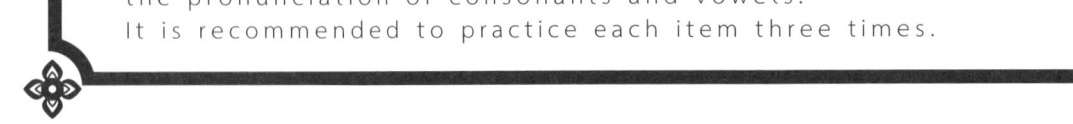

	書寫 Writing	意思 Meaning
11. ทำ		
12. เทา		
13. พอ		
14. ยำ		
15. คอ		
16. รำ		
17. ไว		
18. เรา		
19. งา		
20. ง		

低音子音與母音：選擇題練習

請從以下選項中選擇正確的泰文單字或發音

Multiple Choice Practice
Please select the correct Thai word or pronunciation from the options below.

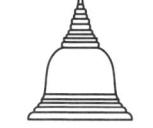

1. 表示「話語」的單字是
   The word for "Words" is
   a) คำ　　　b) คะ　　　c) คอ　　　d) มา

2. 表示「來」的單字是
   The word for "Come" is
   a) มา　　　b) มี　　　c) เงา　　　d) เท

3. 「คือ」的正確發音是
   The correct pronunciation of "คือ" is
   a) khue:1　　b) kue:1　　c) chue:1　　d) sue:1

4. 表示「紅毛丹」的單字是
   The word for "Rambutan" is
   a) เงาะ　　b) แพะ　　c) งู　　d) เงา

5. 「แพะ」的意思是
   The word for "แพะ" is
   a) 山羊 goat.　b) 牛 Cow　c) 馬 Horse　d) 豬 Pig

6. 「เงา」的正確發音是
   The correct pronunciation of "เงา" is
   a) ngao1　　b) kao1　　c) mao1　　d) tao1

7. 表示「藥」的單字是
   The word for "Medicine" is
   a) ยา　　　b) ย่ำ　　　c) งา　　　d) นา

低音子音與母音：選擇題練習

請從以下選項中選擇正確的泰文單字或發音
Multiple Choice Practice
Please select the correct Thai word or pronunciation from the options below.

8. 「ทำ」的意思是
The word for "ทำ" is
 a) 做 do b) 看 look c) 拿 take d) 吃 eat

9. 「พา」的正確發音是
The correct pronunciation of "พา" is
 a) pha:1 b) ba:1 c) ma:1 d) wa:1

10. 表示「稻田」的單字是
The word for "Rice paddy" is
 a) นา b) เงา c) เงาะ d) เทา

11. 「มี」的意思是
The word for "There is" is
 a) 沒有 don't have b) 有 have c) 買 buy d) 賣 sell

12. 「รำ」的正確發音是
The correct pronunciation of "รำ" is
 a) ram1 b) lam1 c) yam1 d) tam 1

13. 表示「船」的單字是
The word for "Boat" is
 a) แพ b) แพะ c) พอ d) ไว

14. 表示「傾倒」的單字是
The word for "Pour out" is
 a) เท b) พอ c) ทำ d) พา

15. 「งู」的正確發音是
The correct pronunciation of "งู" is
 a) ngu:1 b) ku:1 c) mu:1 d) ru:1

尾音、簡化母音：拼讀練習 MP3 10-01

說明：
請大聲朗讀以下單字與詞組，注意尾音與簡化母音的發音。
建議每題反覆練習3次。

Final Sound, Simplified Vowels: Phonics Practice
Instructions:
Please read the following words and phrases aloud, paying attention to the pronunciation of consonants and vowels.
It is recommended to practice each item three times.

	書寫 Writing	意思 Meaning
1. จบ		
2. พบ		
3. จัด		
4. รับ		
5. ผล		
6. คัด		
7. กิน		
8. บิน		
9. วาง		
10. กัน		

尾音、簡化母音：拼讀練習

說明：
請大聲朗讀以下單字與詞組，注意尾音與簡化母音的發音。
建議每題反覆練習3次。

Final Sound, Simplified Vowels: Phonics Practice
Instructions:
Please read the following words and phrases aloud, paying attention to the pronunciation of consonants and vowels.
It is recommended to practice each item three times.

	書寫 Writing	意思 Meaning
11. รัก	_____	_____
12. งบ	_____	_____
13. บาท	_____	_____
14. บอก	_____	_____
15. เรียน	_____	_____
16. คำ	_____	_____
17. วัน	_____	_____
18. คม	_____	_____
19. ลบ	_____	_____
20. พับ	_____	

尾音、簡化母音：選擇題

請從以下選項中選擇正確的泰文單字或發音
Multiple Choice Practice
Please select the correct Thai word or pronunciation from the options below.

1. 表示「結束」的單字是
The word for "Finish" is
  a) จบ   b) พบ   c) จัด   d) กัน

2. 表示「遇見」的單字是
The word for "Meet" is
  a) พบ   b) พอ   c) พับ   d) ผล

3. 「จัด」的正確發音是
The correct pronunciation of "จัด" is
  a) jat2   b) chat2   c) kat2   d) tat2

4. 表示「學生」的單字是
The word for "Student" is
  a) นักเรียน   b) วัน   c) คำ   d) ผล

5. 「รับ」的正確發音是
The correct pronunciation of "รับ" is
  a) rap4   b) lap4   c) kap4   d) sap4

6. 「วาง」的正確發音是
The correct pronunciation of "รับ" is
  a) wa:ng1   b) ta:ng1   c) sa:ng1   d) ra:ng1

7. 表示「吃」的單字是
The word for "Eat" is
  a) กิน   b) บิน   c) กัน   d) วัน

尾音、簡化母音：選擇題

請從以下選項中選擇正確的泰文單字或發音

Multiple Choice Practice

Please select the correct Thai word or pronunciation from the options below.

8.「บิน」的意思是
The meaning of "บิน" is
 a) 跑 run   b) 飛 fly   c) 走 walk   d) 跳 jump

9.「พอ」的正確發音是
The correct pronunciation of "พอ" is
 a) phor:1   b) por:1   c) thor:1   d) kor:1

10. 表示「愛」的單字是
The word for "Love" is
 a) รัก   b) รับ   c) ชอบ   d) เรียน

11.「งบ」的意思是
The word for "งบ" is
 a) 預算 budget b) 書 book   c) 時間 time   d) 食物 food

12.「บาท」的正確發音是
The correct pronunciation of "บาท" is
 a) ba:t2   b) pa:t2   c) ka:t2   d) wa:t2

13. 表示「告訴」的單字是
The word for "Tell" is
 a) บอก   b) บาท   c) พับ   d) ลบ

14.「เรียน」的意思是
The meaning of "เรียน" is
 a) 寫 write   b) 讀 read   c) 學習 learn   d) 畫 draw

15.「คำ」的正確發音是
The correct pronunciation of "คำ" is
 a) kham1   b) kam1   c) tham1   d) sam 1

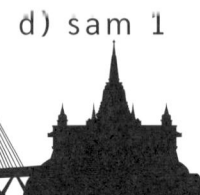

聲調：拼讀練習 MP3 11-01

說明：
請大聲朗讀以下單字與詞組，注意聲調的發音。
建議每題反覆練習3次。

Tone Consonants and Vowels: Phonics Practice
Instructions:
Please read the following words and phrases aloud, paying attention to the pronunciation of consonants and vowels.
It is recommended to practice each item three times.

	書寫 Writing	意思 Meaning
1. บ้าน	___	___
2. ใหญ่	___	___
3. เล่น	___	___
4. ร้อง	___	___
5. ส้ม	___	___
6. เก่า	___	___
7. กุ้ง	___	___
8. ช้าง	___	___
9. นั่ง	___	___
10. อ่าน	___	___

聲調：拼讀練習

說明：
請大聲朗讀以下單字與詞組，注意聲調的發音。
建議每題反覆練習3次。

Tone Consonants and Vowels: Phonics Practice
Instructions:
Please read the following words and phrases aloud, paying attention to the pronunciation of consonants and vowels.
It is recommended to practice each item three times.

	書寫 Writing	意思 Meaning
11. น้อย		
12. บ่น		
13. อ้วน		
14. ตื่น		
15. ข้าว		
16. ว่า		
17. แม่		
18. เก้าอี้		
19. ดอกไม้		
20. น้ำ		

聲調：拼讀練習

說明：
請大聲朗讀以下單字與詞組，注意聲調的發音。
建議每題反覆練習3次。

Tone Consonants and Vowels: Phonics Practice
Instructions:
Please read the following words and phrases aloud, paying attention to the pronunciation of consonants and vowels.
It is recommended to practice each item three times.

書寫 Writing	意思 Meaning
21. ช้า	
22. เลี้ยง	
23. ซื้อ	
24. อื่น	
25. ไม่	

時時泰工作室 | 泰語學習與跨文化交流領導品牌

聲調：選擇題

請從以下選項中選擇正確的泰文單字或發音

Multiple Choice Practice

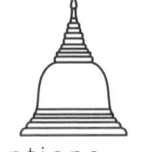

Please select the correct Thai word or pronunciation from the options below.

1. 表示「房子」的單字是
   The word for "House" is
   a) บ้าน   b) ช้าง   c) น้ำ   d) ส้ม

2. 表示「大」的單字是
   The word for "Big" is
   a) เล่น   b) ใหญ่   c) น้อย   d) ช้า

3. 表示「玩」的單字是
   The word for "Play" is
   a) เล่น   b) ร้อง   c) เก่า   d) เลี้ยง

4. 表示「哭」的單字是
   The word for "Cry" is
   a) ร้อง   b) ส้ม   c) บ่น   d) ว่า

5. 表示「橙子」的單字是
   The word for "Orange" is
   a) น้ำ   b) กุ้ง   c) ดอกไม้   d) ส้ม

6. 表示「舊」的單字是
   The word for "Old" is
   a) เก่า   b) เก้าอี้   c) ช้าง   d) อื่น

7. 表示「蝦」的單字是
   The word for "Shrimp" is
   a) ช้า   b) กุ้ง   c) นั่ง   d) ข้าว

時時泰工作室｜ 泰語學習與跨文化交流領導品牌

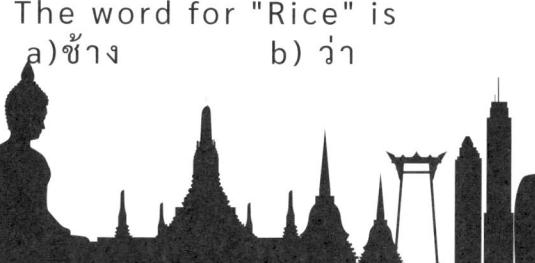

聲調：選擇題

請從以下選項中選擇正確的泰文單字或發音
Multiple Choice Practice
Please select the correct Thai word or pronunciation from the options below.

8. 表示「大象」的單字是
The word for "Elephant" is
   a) ช้าง   b) แม่   c) ซื้อ   d) อ้วน

9. 表示「坐」的單字是
The word for "Sit" is
   a) นั่ง   b) อ่าน   c) ตื่น   d) เลี้ยง

10. 表示「讀」的單字是
The word for "Read" is
   a) น้อย   b) อ่าน   c) บ่น   d) ว่า

11. 表示「少」的單字是
The word for "Little" is
   a) อ้วน   b) น้อย   c) ใหญ่   d) ช้า

12. 表示「抱怨」的單字是
The word for "Complain" is
   a) แม่   b) ข้าว   c) บ่น   d) ไม่

13. 表示「胖」的單字是
The word for "Chubby" is
   a) อ้วน   b) ตื่น   c) เก้าอี้   d) ดอกไม้

14. 表示「醒來」的單字是
The word for "Wake up" is
   a) ซื้อ   b) น้ำ   c) ตื่น   d) อื่น

15. 表示「米飯」的單字是
The word for "Rice" is
   a) ช้าง   b) ว่า   c) เลี้ยง   d) ข้าว

聲調：選擇題

請從以下選項中選擇正確的泰文單字或發音
Multiple Choice Practice
Please select the correct Thai word or pronunciation from the options below.

16. 表示「說」的單字是
The word for "Say" is
 a) ว่า b) แม่ c) ไม่ d) เก่า

17. 表示「母親」的單字是
The word for "Mother" is
 a) แม่ b) เก้าอี้ c) ดอกไม้ d) อ่าน

18. 表示「椅子」的單字是
The word for "Chair" is
 a) เก้าอี้ b) น้ำ c) ช้า d) กุ้ง

19. 表示「花」的單字是
The word for "Flower" is
 a) ดอกไม้ b) เล่น c) ร้อง d) บ่น

20. 表示「不」的單字是
The word for "Not" is
 a) ไม่ b) ว่า c) อื่น d) ตื่น

前引字：拼讀練習　MP3 12-01

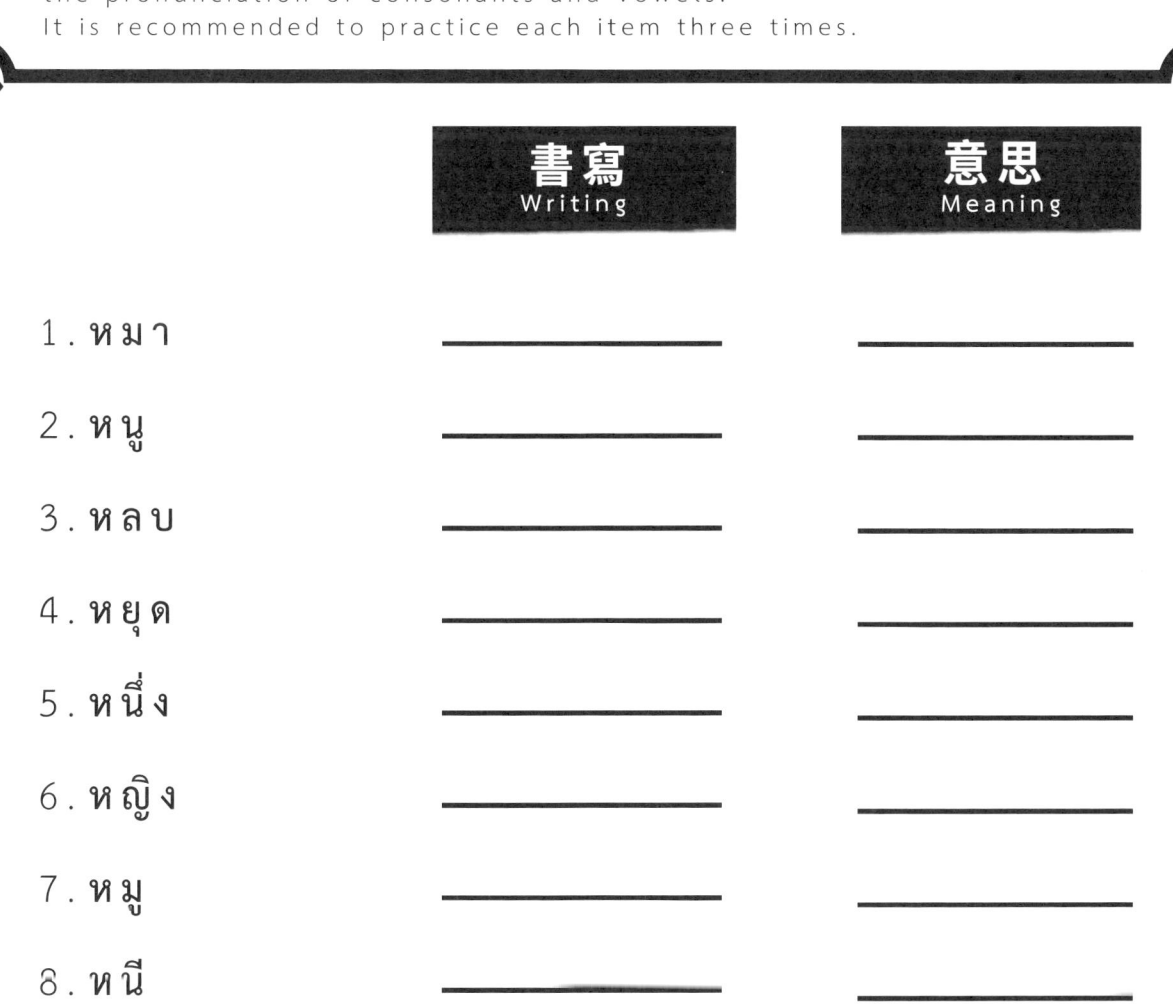

說明：
請大聲朗讀以下單字與詞組，注意前引字的發音。
建議每題反覆練習3次。

Leading consonant: Phonics Practice
Instructions:
Please read the following words and phrases aloud, paying attention to the pronunciation of consonants and vowels.
It is recommended to practice each item three times.

書寫 Writing	意思 Meaning

1. หมา
2. หนู
3. หลบ
4. หยุด
5. หนึ่ง
6. หญิง
7. หมู
8. หนี
9. หมอ
10. หนาว

前引字：拼讀練習

說明：
請大聲朗讀以下單字與詞組，注意前引字的發音。
建議每題反覆練習3次。

Leading consonant: Phonics Practice
Instructions:
Please read the following words and phrases aloud, paying attention to the pronunciation of consonants and vowels.
It is recommended to practice each item three times.

	書寫 Writing	意思 Meaning
11. หนา		
12. หรู		
13. หนอน		
14. หมด		
15. หนุ่ม		
16. หยาด		
17. หมาย		
18. หมึก		
19. หนังสือ		
20. หม้อ		

前引字：拼讀練習

說明：
請大聲朗讀以下單字與詞組，注意前引字的發音。
建議每題反覆練習3次。

Leading consonant: Phonics Practice
Instructions:
Please read the following words and phrases aloud, paying attention to the pronunciation of consonants and vowels.
It is recommended to practice each item three times.

	書寫 Writing	意思 Meaning
21. หนู	_____	_____
22. ห่ม	_____	_____
23. หวัง	_____	_____
24. หมอก	_____	_____
25. หนอง	_____	_____

前引字：選擇題

請從以下選項中選擇正確的泰文單字或發音
Multiple Choice Practice
Please select the correct Thai word or pronunciation from the options below.

1. 表示「狗」的單字是
The word for "Dog" is
 a) หมา b) หมู c) หนู d) หมอ

2. 表示「老鼠」的單字是
The word for "Mouse " is
 a) หนู b) หนอน c) หนา d) หนุ่ม

3. 表示「停止」的單字是
The word for "Stop" is
 a) หวัง b) หยาด c) หยุด d) หนอง

4. 表示「一」的單字是
The word for "One" is
 a) หนึ่ง b) หนอง c) หนาว d) หนี

5. 表示「女人」的單字是
The word for "Woman" is
 a) หมอก b) หนุ่ม c) หญิง d) หมึก

6. 表示「豬」的單字是
The word for "Pig" is
 a) หม้อ b) หมา c) หมอ d) หมู

7. 表示「逃跑」的單字是
The word for "Run away" is
 a) หนี b) หนา c) หนอง d) หนอน

8. 表示「醫生」的單字是
The word for "Doctor" is
 a) หมอ b) หมา c) หมึก d) หมอก

前引字：選擇題

請從以下選項中選擇正確的泰文單字或發音

Multiple Choice Practice
Please select the correct Thai word or pronunciation from the options below.

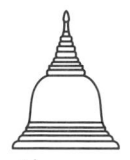

9. 表示「冷」的單字是
The word for "Cold" is
 a) หนาว	b) หนา	c) หนู	d) หนุ่ม

10. 表示「厚」的單字是
The word for "Thick" is
 a) หนี	b) หนา	c) หนอน	d) หนอง

11. 表示「豪華」的單字是
The word for "Luxury" is
 a) หมอก	b) หรู	c) หมัก	d) หม้อ

12. 表示「蟲」的單字是
The word for "Worm" is
 a) หนอน	b) หนู	c) หนาว	d) หนา

13. 表示「用完」的單字是
The word for "Used up " is
 a) หมด	b) หยุด	c) หยาด	d) หวัง

14. 表示「年輕男人」的單字是
The word for "Young man" is
 a) หญิง	b) หนุ่ม	c) หนี	d) หนอง

15. 表示「露水」的單字是
The word for "Dew" is
 a) หยาด	b) หยุด	c) หมอก	d) หมัก

前引字：選擇題

請從以下選項中選擇正確的泰文單字或發音

Multiple Choice Practice

Please select the correct Thai word or pronunciation from the options below.

16. 表示「號碼」的單字是
The word for "Number" is
 a) หมา　　　b) หมายเลข　　　c) หม้อ　　　d) หมึก

17. 表示「墨水」的單字是
The word for "Ink" is
 a) หมึก　　　b) หมอก　　　c) หมัก　　　d) หมอ

18. 表示「鍋」的單字是
The word for "Pot" is
 a) หมู　　　b) หมา　　　c) หม้อ　　　d) หมอ

19. 表示「蓋（被子）」的單字是
The word for "Cover (with a blanket)" is
 a) ห่ม　　　b) หวัง　　　c) หยาด　　　d) หยุด

20. 表示「希望」的單字是
The word for "Hope" is
 a) หนอง　　　b) หมอก　　　c) หมัก　　　d) หวัง

短句拼讀一：拼讀練習

MP3 13-01

說明：
請大聲讀出以下短句，注意每個單字的發音與聲調
建議每題反覆練習3次。

Short Sentence Reading 1: Phonics Practice
Instructions:
Please read aloud the following short sentences. Pay attention to the pronunciation and tones of each word.

	書寫 Writing	意思 Meaning
1. ฉันกลับบ้าน		
2. แมวนั่งบนโต๊ะ		
3. เขาเลี้ยงหมู		
4. ฉันอ่านหนังสือ		
5. เด็กกินข้าว		

短句拼讀一：拼讀練習

說明：
請大聲讀出以下短句，注意每個單字的發音與聲調
建議每題反覆練習3次。

Short Sentence Reading 1: Phonics Practice
Instructions:
Please read aloud the following short sentences. Pay attention to the pronunciation and tones of each word.

	書寫 Writing	意思 Meaning
6. แม่ซื้อส้ม	____	____
7. เขาถามคำถาม	____	____
8. ฉันชอบกุ้ง	____	____
9. ช้างเดินช้า	____	____
10. ฉันคิดว่า	____	____

短句拼讀一：拼讀練習

說明：
請大聲讀出以下短句，注意每個單字的發音與聲調
建議每題反覆練習3次。

Short Sentence Reading 1: Phonics Practice
Instructions:
Please read aloud the following short sentences. Pay attention to the pronunciation and tones of each word.

	書寫 Writing	意思 Meaning
11. เขาทำงาน		
12. เด็กตัวเล็ก		
13. คนมาก		
14. บ้านใหญ่		
15. นักเรียนเรียนภาษาไทย		

短句拼讀一：拼讀練習

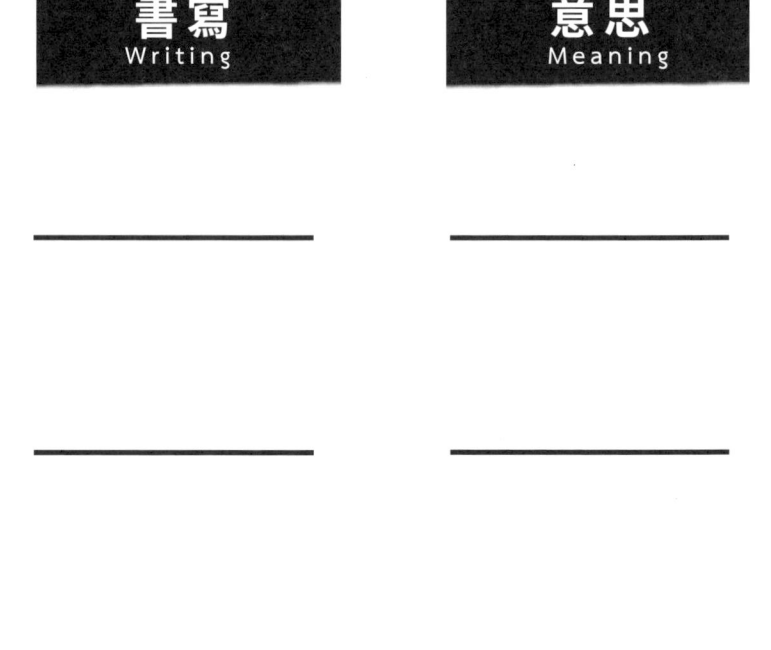

說明：
請大聲讀出以下短句，注意每個單字的發音與聲調
建議每題反覆練習3次。

Short Sentence Reading 1: Phonics Practice
Instructions:
Please read aloud the following short sentences. Pay attention to the pronunciation and tones of each word.

	書寫 Writing	意思 Meaning
16. เด็กเล่นที่สนาม		
17. ฉันอ่านหนังสือ		
18. แม่นั่งบนเก้าอี้		
19. เขาร้องเพลง		
20. ข้าวน้อย		

短句拼讀一：拼讀練習

說明：
請大聲讀出以下短句，注意每個單字的發音與聲調
建議每題反覆練習3次。

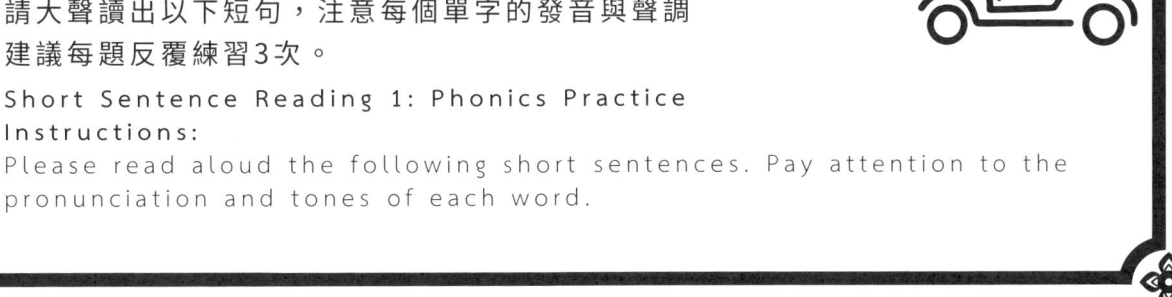

Short Sentence Reading 1: Phonics Practice
Instructions:
Please read aloud the following short sentences. Pay attention to the pronunciation and tones of each word.

	書寫 Writing	意思 Meaning
21.นักเรียนเก่ง		
22.ดอกไม้สวย		
23.เขาอ้วนมาก		
24.เธอผอม		
25.เขียนจดหมาย		

短句拼讀一：拼讀練習

說明：
請大聲讀出以下短句，注意每個單字的發音與聲調
建議每題反覆練習3次。

Short Sentence Reading 1: Phonics Practice
Instructions:
Please read aloud the following short sentences. Pay attention to the pronunciation and tones of each word.

	書寫 Writing	意思 Meaning
26. เด็กอาบน้ำ		
27. ฉันเห็นควาย		
28. เขาตื่นเช้า		
29. ฉันเจ็บมือ		
30. หนังสือเก่า		

短句拼讀一：拼讀練習

說明：
請大聲讀出以下短句，注意每個單字的發音與聲調
建議每題反覆練習3次。

Short Sentence Reading 1: Phonics Practice
Instructions:
Please read aloud the following short sentences. Pay attention to the pronunciation and tones of each word.

	書寫 Writing	意思 Meaning
36. เขาทราบข่าวดี		
37. ฉันกินข้าวกับเพื่อน		
38. นกบินในท้องฟ้า		
39. พอแล้วขอบคุณ		
40. เขารักครอบครัวมาก		

短句拼讀一：拼讀練習

說明：
請大聲讀出以下短句，注意每個單字的發音與聲調
建議每題反覆練習3次。

Short Sentence Reading 1: Phonics Practice
Instructions:
Please read aloud the following short sentences. Pay attention to the pronunciation and tones of each word.

	書寫 Writing	意思 Meaning
41. งบประมาณของปีนี้		
42. แม่บอกให้ทำการบ้าน		
43. พ่อบ่นเรื่องงาน		
44. ฉันเรียนรู้คำใหม่		
45. วันนี้อากาศดี		

短句拼讀一：拼讀練習

說明：
請大聲讀出以下短句，注意每個單字的發音與聲調
建議每題反覆練習3次。

Short Sentence Reading 1: Phonics Practice
Instructions:
Please read aloud the following short sentences. Pay attention to the pronunciation and tones of each word.

	書寫 Writing	意思 Meaning
46. มีดคมมาก	_____	_____
47. กรุณาลบข้อความนี้	_____	_____
48. เขาพับเสื้อผ้า	_____	_____
49. ฉันรับจดหมาย	_____	_____
50. ฉันวางหนังสือบนโต๊ะ	_____	_____

短句拼讀二：拼讀練習 MP3 13-02

說明：
請大聲讀出以下短句，注意每個單字的發音與聲調
建議每題反覆練習3次。

Short Sentence Reading 2: Phonics Practice
Instructions:
Please read aloud the following short sentences. Pay attention to the pronunciation and tones of each word.

	書寫 Writing	意思 Meaning
1. สุนัขวิ่งเร็ว		
2. หนูกินข้าว		
3. หมูนอนในกรง		
4. เขาหยุดทำงาน		
5. ฉันมีเงินหนึ่งบาท		

短句拼讀二：拼讀練習

說明：
請大聲讀出以下短句，注意每個單字的發音與聲調
建議每題反覆練習3次。

Short Sentence Reading 2: Phonics Practice
Instructions:
Please read aloud the following short sentences. Pay attention to the pronunciation and tones of each word.

	書寫 Writing	意思 Meaning
6. ผู้หญิงสวยมาก		
7. หมอรักษาคนป่วย		
8. เด็กหนีจากบ้าน		
9. อากาศหนาวมาก		
10. หนังสือหนา		

短句拼讀二：拼讀練習

說明：
請大聲讀出以下短句，注意每個單字的發音與聲調
建議每題反覆練習3次。

Short Sentence Reading 2: Phonics Practice
Instructions:
Please read aloud the following short sentences. Pay attention to the pronunciation and tones of each word.

	書寫 Writing	意思 Meaning
11. บ้านหรู		
12. หนอนกินใบไม้		
13. น้ำหยุดไหล		
14. เขาหยาดเหงื่อ		
15. หมดเวลาแล้ว		

短句拼讀二：拼讀練習

說明：
請大聲讀出以下短句，注意每個單字的發音與聲調
建議每題反覆練習3次。

Short Sentence Reading 2: Phonics Practice
Instructions:
Please read aloud the following short sentences. Pay attention to the pronunciation and tones of each word.

	書寫 Writing	意思 Meaning
16. ชายหนุ่มนั่งใต้ต้นไม้		
17. ฉันมีหมาย		
18. หนีไปที่ไกล		
19. หยุดทำแบบนี้		
20. หมอมาถึงแล้ว		

短句拼讀二：拼讀練習

說明：
請大聲讀出以下短句，注意每個單字的發音與聲調
建議每題反覆練習3次。

Short Sentence Reading 2: Phonics Practice
Instructions:
Please read aloud the following short sentences. Pay attention to the pronunciation and tones of each word.

	書寫 Writing	意思 Meaning
21. หม้ออยู่ในห้องครัว		
22. หนูชอบชีส		
23. แม่ห่มผ้าให้		
24. ฉันหวังว่าจะได้งานดี		
25. หมอกหนามาก		

短句拼讀二：拼讀練習

說明：
請大聲讀出以下短句，注意每個單字的發音與聲調
建議每題反覆練習3次。

Short Sentence Reading 2: Phonics Practice
Instructions:
Please read aloud the following short sentences. Pay attention to the pronunciation and tones of each word.

	書寫 Writing	意思 Meaning
26. หนองน้ำนี้ใหญ่		
27. หลีกไปดีกว่า		
28. ฉันชอบหมักปลา		
29. หมอนหนุนนุ่ม		
30. เขาหลงทาง		

短句拼讀二：拼讀練習

說明：
請大聲讀出以下短句，注意每個單字的發音與聲調
建議每題反覆練習3次。

Short Sentence Reading 2: Phonics Practice
Instructions:
Please read aloud the following short sentences. Pay attention to the pronunciation and tones of each word.

	書寫 Writing	意思 Meaning
31.เด็กเล่นที่สนาม		
32.แมวนอนบนโต๊ะ		
33.ฉันอ่านหนังสือ		
34.แม่ซื้อส้มให้		
35.เขาถามคำถาม		

短句拼讀二：拼讀練習

說明：
請大聲讀出以下短句，注意每個單字的發音與聲調
建議每題反覆練習3次。

Short Sentence Reading 2: Phonics Practice
Instructions:
Please read aloud the following short sentences. Pay attention to the pronunciation and tones of each word.

	書寫 Writing	意思 Meaning
36. ฉันชอบกุ้งมาก		
37. ช้างเดินช้า		
38. เขาคิดว่าได้		
39. เขาทำงานหนัก		
40. เด็กตัวเล็กมาก		

短句拼讀二：拼讀練習

說明：
請大聲讀出以下短句，注意每個單字的發音與聲調
建議每題反覆練習3次。

Short Sentence Reading 2: Phonics Practice
Instructions:
Please read aloud the following short sentences. Pay attention to the pronunciation and tones of each word.

	書寫 Writing	意思 Meaning
41. บ้านใหญ่สวย		
42. นักเรียนเรียนเก่ง		
43. ดอกไม้สวยมาก		
44. เขาอ้วนมาก		
45. เธอผอมลง		

短句拼讀二：拼讀練習

說明：
請大聲讀出以下短句，注意每個單字的發音與聲調
建議每題反覆練習3次。

Short Sentence Reading 2: Phonics Practice
Instructions:
Please read aloud the following short sentences. Pay attention to the pronunciation and tones of each word.

	書寫 Writing	意思 Meaning
46. เขียนจดหมายถึงเพื่อน		
47. เด็กอาบน้ำเย็น		
48. ฉันเห็นควายตัวใหญ่		
49. เขาตื่นเช้าทุกวัน		
50. ฉันเจ็บมือขวา		

練習題答案

Practice Question Answers

中音子音與母音
Mid-pitch Consonants and Vowels

拼讀練習

1. บิดา [bi2 da:1] – 父親 – father
2. ปา [pa:1] – 扔 – throw
3. ปะ [pa2] – 補丁 – patch
4. จะ [ja2] – 將要 – will, shall
5. ดู [du:1] – 看 – look, watch
6. ดุ [du2] – 兇 – fierce, ferocious
7. ตี [ti:1] – 打、擊打 – hit, strike
8. จำ [jam1] – 記住 – remember
9. ตา [ta:1] – 眼睛、祖父 – eye, grandfather
10. เตะ [te2] – 踢 – kick
11. ปู [pu:1] – 螃蟹 – crab
12. ปี [pi:1] – 年 – year
13. แกะ [kae2] – 羊 – sheep
14. อาตีปู [a:1 ti:1 pu:1] – 叔叔打螃蟹 – uncle hits crab (phrase)
15. เจอ [jer1] – 遇見、找到 – meet, find
16. เบา [bao1] – 輕 – light, soft
17. ตะ [ta2] – 短促的「ต」音 – short "t" sound
18. อา [a:1] – 叔叔 – uncle
19. เกาะ [kor2] – 島 – island
20. เอา [a:o1] – 拿、想要 – take, want

選擇題練習

1. a)
2. a)
3. a)
4. a)
5. a)
6. a)
7. a)
8. b)
9. a)
10. a)
11. a)
12. c)
13. a)
14. b)
15. a)

高音子音與母音
High-pitch Consonants and Vowels

拼讀練習

1. ขา [kha:5] - 腿 - leg
2. ถือ [thue3] - 拿、持有 - hold, carry
3. ถู [thu:5] - 擦 - wipe, scrub
4. ผา [pha:5] - 懸崖 - cliff
5. เสียใจ [si:a5 jai1] - 難過 - sad, sorry
6. เสือ [sue:a5] - 老虎 - tiger
7. เขา [khao5] - 他/她、山 - he/she, mountain
8. สาขา [sa:5 kha:5] - 分支、分店 - branch, division
9. เสา [sao5] - 柱子 - pole, pillar
10. สา [sa:5] - 適合 - to suit; to fit; to satisfy; to gratify
11. โส [so:5] - 妓女 - prostitute
12. เฉา [chao5] - 乾枯 - wilt, wither
13. สี [si:5] - 顏色 - color
14. ใส [sai5] - 透明、清澈 - clear, transparent
15. หาผี [ha:5 phi:5] - 找鬼 - look for a ghost (phrase)
16. หู [hu:5] - 耳朵 - ear
17. หอ [hor:5] - 塔、宿舍 - tower, dormitory
18. ชี [chi:5] - 尼姑 - nun
19. โผ [pho:5] - 跳躍、急衝 - to leap; to dart
20. แฉ [chae:5] - 透露、展示 - to reveal, disclose

選擇題練習

1. a)
2. a)
3. a)
4. a)
5. b)
6. a)
7. a)
8. b)
9. a)
10. a)
11. a)
12. a)
13. a)
14. b)
15. c)

低音子音與母音
Low-pitch Consonants and Vowels

拼讀練習

1. คำ [kham1] - 話語、詞 - word, speech
2. ยา [ya:1] - 藥 - medicine
3. มา [ma:1] - 來 - come
4. คือ [khue:1] - 是 - is, be
5. เงาะ [ngor4] - 紅毛丹 - rambutan
6. ใย [yai1] - 纖維、絲 - fiber, thread
7. แพะ [phae4] - 山羊 - goat
8. เท [the:1] - 傾倒、倒出 - pour, dump
9. พา [pha:1] - 帶領 - lead, take along
10. เงา [ngao1] - 影子 - shadow
11. ทำ [tham1] - 做 - do, make
12. เทา [thao1] - 灰色 - gray
13. พอ [pho:1] - 足夠 - enough
14. ยำ [yam1] - 泰式沙拉 - Thai spicy salad
15. คอ [kho:1] - 脖子 - neck
16. รำ [ram1] - 傳統舞蹈 - traditional dance
17. ไว [wai1] - 快 - fast, quick
18. เรา [rao1] - 我們 - we, us
19. งา [nga:1] - 芝麻 - sesame
20. งู [ngu:1] - 蛇 - snake

選擇題練習

1. a)
2. a)
3. a)
4. a)
5. a)
6. a)
7. a)
8. a)
9. a)
10. a)
11. b)
12. a)
13. a)
14. a)
15. a)

尾音、簡化母音
Final sounds, simplified vowels

拼讀練習

1. จบ [jop2] - 結束 - finish, end
2. พบ [phop4] - 遇見 - meet, encounter
3. จัด [jat2] - 整理、安排 - organize, arrange
4. รับ [rap4] - 接受、拿 - receive, accept
5. ผล [phon5] - 結果 - result
6. คัด [khat4] - 挑選、抄寫 - select, copy
7. กิน [kin1] - 吃 - eat
8. บิน [bin1] - 飛 - fly
9. วาง [wa:ng1] - 放置 - place, put
10. กัน [kan1] - 互相 - together, mutually
11. รัก [rak4] - 愛 - love
12. งบ [ngop4] - 預算 - budget
13. บาท [ba:t2] - 泰銖（貨幣單位）- baht (Thai currency)
14. บอก [bo:k2] - 告訴 - tell, inform
15. เรียน [ri:an1] - 學習 - study, learn
16. คำ [kham1] - 詞、話語 - word, speech
17. วัน [wan1] - 天 - day
18. คม [khom1] - 鋒利 - sharp
19. ลบ [lop4] - 擦掉、刪除 - erase, delete
20. พับ [phap4] - 摺疊 - fold

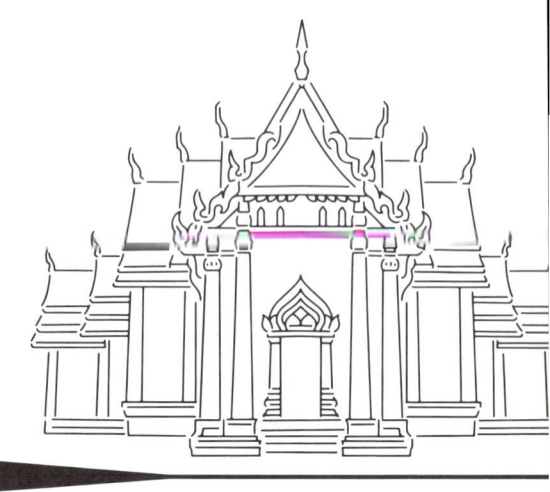

選擇題練習

1. a)
2. a)
3. a)
4. a)
5. a)
6. a)
7. a)
8. b)
9. a)
10. a)
11. a)
12. a)
13. a)
14. c)
15. a)

聲調
Tone

拼讀練習　　　　　　　　　　　　　　選擇題練習

1. บ้าน [ba:n3] - 房子 - house　　　　　1. a)
2. ใหญ่ [yai2] - 大 - big　　　　　　　　2. b)
3. เล่น [len3] - 玩 - play　　　　　　　　3. a)
4. ร้อง [ro:ng4] - 哭、唱 - cry, sing　　4. a)
5. ส้ม [so:m3] - 橙子 - orange　　　　　5. d)
6. เก่า [kao2] - 舊 - old　　　　　　　　6. a)
7. กุ้ง [kung3] - 蝦 - shrimp　　　　　　7. b)
8. ช้าง [cha:ng4] - 大象 - elephant　　 8. a)
9. นั่ง [na:ng3] - 坐 - sit　　　　　　　　9. a)
10. อ่าน [a:n2] - 讀 - read　　　　　　 10. b)
11. น้อย [nor:i4] - 少 - little, few　　 11. b)
12. บ่น [bon2] - 抱怨 - complain　　　 12. c)
13. อ้วน [uan3] - 胖 - fat　　　　　　　13. a)
14. ตื่น [tuen2] - 醒來 - wake up　　　14. c)
15. ข้าว [khao3] - 米飯 - rice　　　　　15. d)
16. ว่า [wa:3] - 說 - say　　　　　　　　16. a)
17. แม่ [mae:3] - 母親 - mother　　　　17. a)
18. เก้าอี้ [kao3 i:3] - 椅子 - chair　　　18. a)
19. ดอกไม้ [dok2 mai4] - 花 - flower　19. a)
20. น้ำ [nam4] - 水 - water　　　　　　20. a)
21. ช้า [cha:4] - 慢 - slow
22. เลี้ยง [li:ang4] - 養、請客 - raise, treat (to a meal)
23. ซื้อ [sue:4] - 買 - buy
24. อื่น [ue:n2] - 其他 - other
25. ไม่ [mai3] - 不 - not

前引字
Leading Consonants Practice

拼讀練習

1. หมา [ma:5] - 狗 - dog
2. หนู [nu:5] - 老鼠 - mouse, rat
3. หลบ [lop2] - 躲藏 - hide
4. หยุด [yut2] - 停止 - stop
5. หนึ่ง [nueng2] - 一 - one
6. หญิง [ying5] - 女人 - woman
7. หมู [mu:5] - 豬 - pig
8. หนี [ni:5] - 逃跑 - escape, flee
9. หมอ [mo:5] - 醫生 - doctor
10. หนาว [nao5] - 冷 - cold
11. หนา [na:5] - 厚 - thick
12. หรู [ru:5] - 豪華 - luxurious
13. หนอน [nor:n5] - 蟲 - worm
14. หมด [mot2] - 用完 - run out, finish
15. หนุ่ม [num2] - 年輕男人 - young man
16. หยาด [ya:t2] - 露水 - dew
17. หมาย [ma:i5] - 意思 - meaning
18. หมึก [muek2] - 墨水 - ink
19. หนังสือ [nang:5 sue:5] - 書 - book
20. หม้อ [mo:3] - 鍋 - pot
21. หนู [nu:5] - 老鼠 - mouse, rat
22. ห่ม [hom2] - 蓋（被子）- cover (with blanket)
23. หวัง [wang5] - 希望 - hope
24. หมอก [mo:k2] - 霧 - fog
25. หนอง [no:ng5] - 沼澤 - swamp, marsh

選擇題練習

1. a)
2. a)
3. c)
4. a)
5. c)
6. d)
7. a)
8. a)
9. a)
10. b)
11. b)
12. a)
13. a)
14. b)
15. a)
16. b)
17. a)
18. c)
19. a)
20. d)

短句拼讀一：拼讀練習
Short Sentence Phonics 1: Phonics Practice

1. ฉันกลับบ้าน [chan5 klap2 ba:n3] - 我回家 - I go back home
2. แมวนั่งบนโต๊ะ [maew1 nang3 bon1 to4] - 貓坐在桌子上 - The cat sits on the table
3. เขาเลี้ยงหมู [khao5 li:ang5 mu:5] - 他養豬 - He raises pigs
4. ฉันอ่านหนังสือ [chan5 a:n2 nang5 sue5] - 我讀書 - I read a book
5. เด็กกินข้าว [dek2 kin1 khao3] - 小孩吃飯 - The child eats rice
6. แม่ซื้อส้ม [mae3 sue:4 so:m3] - 媽媽買橙子 - Mother buys oranges
7. เขาถามคำถาม [khao5 tha:m5 kham1 tha:m5] - 他問問題 - He asks a question
8. ฉันชอบกุ้ง [chan5 cho:p3 kung3] - 我喜歡蝦 - I like shrimp
9. ช้างเดินช้า [cha:ng4 der:n1 cha:4] - 大象走得慢 - The elephant walks slowly
10. ฉันคิดว่า [chan5 khit4 wa:3] - 我認為 - I think that
11. เขาทำงาน [khao5 tham1 nga:n1] - 他工作 - He works
12. เด็กตัวเล็ก [dek2 tu:a1 lek4] - 小孩很小 - The child is small
13. คนมาก [khon1 ma:k3] - 人很多 - There are many people
14. บ้านใหญ่ [ba:n3 yai2] - 房子很大 - The house is big
15. นักเรียนเรียนภาษาไทย [na:k4 ri:an1 ri:an1 pha:1sa:5thai1] -
16. 學生學習泰語 - Students learn Thai
17. เด็กเล่นที่สนาม [dek2 len3 thi:3 sa2na:m5] - 小孩在操場玩 - Children play at the playground
18. ฉันอ่านหนังสือ [chan5 a:n2 nang5 sue:5] - 我讀書 - I read a book
19. แม่นั่งบนเก้าอี้ [mae3 nang3 bon1 kao3 i:3] - 媽媽坐在椅子上 - Mother sits on the chair
20. เขาร้องเพลง [khao5 ro:ng4 phle:ng1] - 他唱歌 - He sings a song
21. ข้าวน้อย [khao3 nor:i4] - 米飯很少 - There is little rice
22. นักเรียนเก่ง [na:k4 ri:an1 keng2] - 學生很聰明 - The student is smart
23. ดอกไม้สวย [do:k2 mai4 suai5] - 花很漂亮 - The flower is beautiful
24. เขาอ้วนมาก [khao3 u:an3 ma:k3] - 他很胖 - He is very fat
25. เธอผอม [ther1 pho:m5] - 她很瘦 - She is thin
26. เขียนจดหมาย [khi:an5 jot2 ma:i5] - 寫信 - Write a letter

94

短句拼讀一：拼讀練習
Short Sentence Phonics 1: Phonics Practice

26. เด็กอาบน้ำ [dek2 a:p2 nam4] - 小孩洗澡 - The child takes a bath
27. ฉันเห็นควาย [chan5 hen5 khwa:i1] - 我看見水牛 - I see a buffalo
28. เขาตื่นเช้า [khao5 tuen2 chao4] - 他早上醒來 - He wakes up in the morning
29. ฉันเจ็บมือ [chan5 jep2 mue1] - 我的手痛 - My hand hurts
30. หนังสือเก่า [nang5 sue5 kao2] - 書很舊 - The book is old
31. ฉันจบการศึกษา [chan5 jop2 ka:n1 suek2 sa:5] - 我畢業了 - I graduated
32. เราพบกันที่โรงเรียน [rao1 phop2 kan1 thi:3 ro:ng1 ri:an1] - 我們在學校見面 - We meet at school
33. เขาจัดงานปาร์ตี้ [khao5 jat2 nga:n1 pha:1 dti:3] - 他舉辦派對 - He organizes a party
34. นักเรียนตั้งใจเรียน [na:k4 ri:an1 tang3 jai1 ri:an1] - 學生認真學習 - Students study diligently
35. ผลการสอบออกแล้ว [phon5 ka:n1 so:p2 o:k2 laeo4] - 考試結果出來了 - The exam results are out
36. เขาทราบข่าวดี [khao5 sa:p3 khao2 di:1] - 他知道好消息 - He knows good news
37. ฉันกินข้าวกับเพื่อน [chan5 kin1 khao3 kap2 phuean3] - 我和朋友一起吃飯 - I eat rice with friends
38. นกบินในท้องฟ้า [nok4 bin1 nai1 tho:ng4 fa:4] - 鳥在天上飛 - Birds fly in the sky
39. พอแล้วขอบคุณ [phor:1 laeo4 kho:p2 khun1] - 夠了，謝謝 - That's enough, thank you
40. เขารักครอบครัวมาก [khao5 rak4 khro:p3 khrua1 ma:k3] - 他很愛家人 - He loves his family very much
41. งบประมาณของปีนี้ [ngop4 pra1 ma:n1 khor:ng5 pi:1 ni:4] - 今年的預算 - This year's budget
42. แม่บอกให้ทำการบ้าน [mae3 bo:k2 hai3 tham1 ka:n1 ba:n3] - 媽媽叫我做作業 - Mother tells me to do homework
43. พ่อบ่นเรื่องงาน [pho:3 bon2 rue:ang3 nga:n1] - 爸爸抱怨工作 - Father complains about work

95

短句拼讀一：拼讀練習
Short Sentence Phonics 1: Phonics Practice

44. ฉันเรียนรู้คำใหม่ [chan5 ri:an1 ru:4 kham1 mai2] - 我學會了新詞 - I learned a new word
45. วันนี้อากาศดี [wan1 ni:4 a:1 ka:t2 di:1] - 今天天氣很好 - The weather is nice today
46. มีดคมมาก [mi:t3 khom1 ma:k3] - 刀很鋒利 - The knife is very sharp
47. กรุณาลบข้อความนี้ [ka2ru4na:1 lop4 khor:3 khwa:m1 ni:4] - 請刪除這條訊息 - Please delete this message
48. เขาพับเสื้อผ้า [khao5 phap4 suea3 pha:3] - 他摺衣服 - He folds clothes
49. ฉันรับจดหมาย [chan5 rap4 jot2 ma:i5] - 我收到信 - I receive a letter
50. ฉันวางหนังสือบนโต๊ะ [chan5 wa:ng1 nang5 sue5 bon1 to4] - 我把書放在桌子上 - I place the book on the table

短句拼讀二：拼讀練習
Short Sentence Phonics 2: Phonics Practice

1. สุนัขวิ่งเร็ว [su2nak2 wing3 reo1] - 狗跑得很快 - The dog runs very fast
2. หนูกินข้าว [nu:5 kin1 khao3] - 老鼠吃飯 - The mouse eats rice
3. หมูนอนในกรง [mu:5 nor:n1 nai1 krong1] - 豬睡在籠子裡 - The pig sleeps in the cage
4. เขาหยุดทำงาน [khao5 yut2 tham1 nga:n1] - 他停止工作 - He stops working
5. ฉันมีเงินหนึ่งบาท [chan5 mi:1 nger:n1 nueng2 ba:t2] - 我有一泰銖 - I have one baht
6. ผู้หญิงสวยมาก [phu:3 ying5 suai5 ma:k3] - 女人很漂亮 - The woman is very beautiful
7. หมอรักษาคนป่วย [mor:5 rak4 sa:5 khon1 puai2] - 醫生治療病人 - The doctor treats the patient
8. เด็กหนีจากบ้าน [dek2 ni:5 ja:k2 ba:n3] - 小孩從家裡逃跑 - The child escapes from home
9. อากาศหนาวมาก [a:1 ka:t2 nao5 ma:k3] - 天氣很冷 - The weather is very cold
10. หนังสือหนา [nang5 sue:5 na:5] - 書很厚 - The book is thick
11. บ้านหรู [ba:n3 ru:5] - 房子很豪華 - The house is luxurious
12. หนอนกินใบไม้ [nor:n5 kin1 bai1 mai4] - 蟲吃樹葉 - The worm eats leaves
13. น้ำหยุดไหล [na:m4 yut2 lai5] - 水停止流動 - The water stops flowing
14. เขาหยาดเหงื่อ [khao5 ya:t2 nguea2] - 他流汗 - He sweats
15. หมดเวลาแล้ว [mot2 we:1la:1 laeo4] - 時間到了 - Time is up
16. ชายหนุ่มนั่งใต้ต้นไม้ [cha:i1 num2 nang3 tai3 to:n3 mai4] - 年輕男人坐在樹下 - The young man sits under the tree
17. ฉันมีหมาย [chan5 mi:1 ma:i5] - 我有號碼 - I have a number
18. หนีไปที่ไกล [ni:5 pai1 thi:3 klai1] - 逃到遠處 - Escape to a far place
19. หยุดทำแบบนี้ [yut2 tham1 baep2 ni:4] - 停止這樣做 - Stop doing this
20. หมอมาถึงแล้ว [mor:5 ma:1 thung4 laeo4] - 醫生到了 - The doctor has arrived

短句拼讀二：拼讀練習
Short Sentence Phonics 2: Phonics Practice

21. หม้ออยู่ในห้องครัว [mo:3 yu:2 nai1 ho:ng3 khrua1] - 鍋在廚房裡 - The pot is in the kitchen
22. หนูชอบชีส [nu:5 cho:p3 chi:d4] - 老鼠喜歡奶酪 - The mouse likes cheese
23. แม่ห่มผ้าให้ [mae3 hom2 pha:3 hai3] - 媽媽幫我蓋被子 - Mother covers me with a blanket
24. ฉันหวังว่าจะได้งานดี [chan5 wang5 wa:3 ja2 dai3 nga:n1 di:1] - 我希望能得到好工作 - I hope to get a good job
25. หมอกหนามาก [mo:k2 na:5 ma:k3] - 霧很濃 - The fog is very thick
26. หนองน้ำนี้ใหญ่ [nor:ng5 nam4 ni:4 yai2] - 這個沼澤很大 - This swamp is very big
27. หลีกไปดีกว่า [li:k2 pai1 di:1 kwa:2] - 避開比較好 - It's better to avoid
28. ฉันชอบหมักปลา [chan5 chor:p3 mak2 pla:1] - 我喜歡醃魚 - I like pickled fish
29. หมอนหนุนนุ่ม [mor:n5 nun5 num2] - 枕頭很軟 - The pillow is soft
30. เขาหลงทาง [khao5 long5 tha:ng1] - 他迷路了 - He is lost
31. เด็กเล่นที่สนาม [dek2 len3 thi:3 sa2na:m5] - 小孩在操場玩 - Children play at the playground
32. แมวนอนบนโต๊ะ [maew1 nor:n1 bon1 to4] - 貓睡在桌子上 - The cat sleeps on the table
33. ฉันอ่านหนังสือ [chan5 a:n2 nang5sue5] - 我讀書 - I read a book
34. แม่ซื้อส้มให้ [mae3 sue4 so:m3 hai3] - 媽媽買橙子給我 - Mother buys oranges for me
35. เขาถามคำถาม [khao3 tha:m5 kham1 tha:m5] - 他問問題 - He asks a question
36. ฉันชอบกุ้งมาก [chan5 cho:p3 kung3 ma:k3] - 我很喜歡蝦 - I really like shrimp
37. ช้างเดินช้า [cha:ng4 dern1 cha:4] - 大象走得慢 - The elephant walks slowly
38. เขาคิดว่าได้ [khao3 khit4 wa:3 dai3] - 他認為可以 - He thinks it's possible

短句拼讀二：拼讀練習
Short Sentence Phonics 2: Phonics Practice

39. เขาทำงานหนัก [khao5 tham1 nga:n1 nak4] - 他工作很努力 - He works hard
40. เด็กตัวเล็กมาก [dek2 tu:a1 lek4 ma:k3] - 小孩很小 - The child is very small
41. บ้านใหญ่สวย [ba:n3 yai2 suai5] - 房子很大很漂亮 - The house is big and beautiful
42. นักเรียนเรียนเก่ง [nak4 ri:an1 ri:an1 keng2] - 學生學得很棒 - The student studies well
43. ดอกไม้สวยมาก [do:k2 mai4 suai5 ma:k3] - 花很漂亮 - The flower is very beautiful
44. เขาอ้วนมาก [khao5 uan3 ma:k3] - 他很胖 - He is very fat
45. เธอผอมลง [ther1 pho:m5 long1] - 她瘦了 - She has become thin
46. เขียนจดหมายถึงเพื่อน [khi:an5 jot2 ma:i5 thung5 phuean3] - 寫信給朋友 - Write a letter to a friend
47. เด็กอาบน้ำเย็น [dek2 a:p2 nam4 yen1] - 小孩洗冷水澡 - The child takes a cold bath
48. ฉันเห็นควายตัวใหญ่ [chan5 hen5 khwa:i1 tu:a1 yai2] - 我看見大水牛 - I see a big buffalo
49. เขาตื่นเช้าทุกวัน [khao5 tuen2 chao4 thuk4 wan1] - 他每天早上醒來 - He wakes up every morning
50. ฉันเจ็บมือขวา [chan5 jep2 mue1 khwa:5] - 我的右手痛 - My right hand hurts